Cheekbones tha̶͟ supported a gri̶͟ watched. A cleft in his chin and a dimple only on the left side of his smile could only mean one thing.

"You're not—I mean, you didn't because you're. . ." Still gasping for air, Lise lifted her gaze a notch higher to meet the amused stare of her attacker: "Uncle Ted?"

The architect chuckled again. "I supposed I'd answer to that in some circles, but most folks just call me plain old Ted."

She straightened and held one hand to her heaving chest while supporting herself against the door frame with the other. "What in the world were you doing skulking around here? You scared me to death."

He shrugged, his face a mask of boyish innocence beneath dark brows. "Me? Nah, it's that rocking chair you've got to watch out for. From the tussle I witnessed, you're lucky to be alive. You gave it a good go, though, especially when the flames broke out."

Lise looked past him to where the chair in which she'd been relaxing a moment ago now lay on its side. Heat began to climb from her neck into her cheeks as the realization dawned on her.

"The rocking chair? You mean there wasn't a. . ." She paused to collect her thoughts. What an idiot she'd been. "So why exactly are you here?"

KATHLEEN Y'BARBO is a best-selling author of twenty-nine novels, novellas, and young adult books. In all, more than half a million copies of her books are currently in print in the United States and abroad. She has been named as a finalist in the American Christian Fiction Writers Book of the Year contest every year since its inception in 2003, often for more than one book. In addition to her skills as an author, Kathleen is also a publicist at Books & Such Literary Agency. She is a member of the Public Relations Society of America, Words for the Journey Christian Writers Guild, and the Authors Guild. She is also a former treasurer of the American Christian Fiction Writers. A native Texan, Kathleen has three grown sons and a teenage daughter.

Books by Kathleen Y'Barbo

HEARTSONG PRESENTS

HP474—You Can't Buy Love
HP529—Major League Dad
HP571—Bayou Fever
HP659—Bayou Beginnings
HP675—Bayou Secrets
HP691—Bayou Dreams
HP706—The Dwelling Place
HP748—Golden Twilight
HP758—Wedded Bliss

Don't miss out on any of our super romances. Write to us at the following address for information on our newest releases and club information.

Heartsong Presents Readers' Service
PO Box 721
Uhrichsville, OH 44683

Or visit www.heartsongpresents.com

Building Dreams

Kathleen Y'Barbo

Heartsong Presents

To Kathy Ide, who made me promise I would never marry the middleman.

A note from the Author:
I love to hear from my readers! You may correspond with me by writing:

Kathleen Y'Barbo
Author Relations
PO Box 721
Uhrichsville, OH 44683

ISBN 978-1-60260-056-0

BUILDING DREAMS

Our mission is to publish and distribute inspirational products offering exceptional value and biblical encouragement to the masses.

PRINTED IN THE U.S.A.

one

Three hundred—odd years separated Theophile "Ted" Breaux IV from the refugees who'd claimed this section of the bayou for their own, and it had been just over a hundred years since his great-grandfather built the home where he now stood. And yet for all the changes, so much remained the same.

Even with his mother's passing and Pop retired and living out his dream of traveling the world building churches, there was something about this plot of land that made it forever home.

Across the way, Ted could see the building where Grandfather's father, the first Theophile Breaux, had fashioned a schoolhouse from the remains of the original Breaux dwelling. Just last year, the state had finally declared it an official historical site. Thankfully, it would be protected, unlike so much of the town that his family had called home all these generations.

"So much history."

Running his hand across the boards cut from among the cypress that still grew on the property, Ted shook his head. So many others had stood here, had touched the rail as Ted did now.

His architect's eye told him the home had weathered good and bad in less than equal measure. The good always seemed to be what was remembered, the bad only serving to emphasize the blessings when they came.

So many others had looked straight into storms and dared them to try to take the land from them. Now, with one bang of a judge's gavel, the Louisiana legal system could do what no hurricane could. Of course, Ted wouldn't let that happen.

As before, he would pay his brother's debts and keep the home in the family. The check had already been written, and tomorrow he would deliver it on his way back to Baton Rouge. Ted sighed. If only he didn't have to turn his car toward home and work, he'd gladly spend another day or two here in Latagnier.

And yet all he'd worked for and dreamed of waited back in Baton Rouge.

Inside, a television blared to life, most likely the state-of-the-art flat panel that Wyatt just had to have for the room that had once been the home's parlor. A ball game, probably the Saints by the sound of the cheering—and by the sound of Wyatt's complaints.

Abruptly, the roar of the crowd disappeared. "Hey, get in here, T. I know it's only preseason, but your team's actually winning." Wyatt paused to whoop, presumably at the home team. "Or are you too busy staring at the porch posts again?"

Ted turned toward the sound of his younger brother's voice and bit back a retort. If Wyatt cared more about the porch posts—and the home to which they were attached—and less about football, the current situation never would have reached the crisis point.

There was only one thing to do.

He stepped inside and waited for his eyes to adjust then strode to the sofa and snagged the remote. A moment later, Ted pressed the POWER button and the plasma screen went black.

"Hey! What're you doing, man?" Wyatt made a grab for the remote, but Ted easily sidestepped him. Defeated, the younger Breaux slumped against the sofa and held up both hands. "All right. I give up." He relaxed his pose. "What have I done this time?"

Taking his time to answer meant Ted wouldn't throttle his

brother. He inhaled deeply and prayed as he exhaled. "Done?" Another slow breath in and out, another prayer. "Well, Wyatt, let's see." Ted bypassed the modern-looking sofa, likely purchased on one of the many credit cards the kid had run up to its limit, to walk toward the century-old fireplace, still boasting the original millwork. "Ignoring the obvious fact that you've taken Granddad's place—which was given to you at absolutely no cost—"

"Hey now." Wyatt rose and took two steps toward him before stopping to settle for a belligerent look. "You said you didn't want it. Besides, a guy like you doesn't need charity, does he?"

Charity? Obviously, the kid had no clue that living here was a *privilege*, not something to do until a better option came along.

The temper he'd tried to keep under control began to boil. Ted fisted his fingers then wisely stuffed them into his jeans pockets. Wyatt might be ten years younger, but Ted took pride in the fact that he was in no worse shape now than when he'd caught touchdown passes in the NFL.

"No, Wyatt," Ted managed through his clenched jaw, "I said I didn't *need* the place. And I fail to see how being entrusted to carry on the legacy of the Breaux family by living in the home our great-grandfather built is a burden or how it could possibly be considered charity."

His brother's shoulders sagged. "No, I guess you wouldn't," he said as he turned and walked away. A second later, he stopped and glanced back over his shoulder. "But then, you're the one who likes old places. Makes me wonder why you bother living in that glass-and-concrete apartment in Baton Rouge when you're obviously the one who should be back here carrying on the legacy of the Breaux family."

"The Hayes Building is an important midcentury architectural masterpiece, and I'm lucky to have a place there."

Ted paused, painfully aware of how silly the argument must sound to a man whose sole pleasure in life was to seek out and master the latest electronic gadget. While good sense should have kept his mouth shut, bullheadedness kept it in motion. He looked beyond Wyatt and exhaled. "And if there's one thing I can't imagine, it's leaving a job with Hillman & Wright when I'm next in line to be named partner."

A decent argument. Of all the architects in the firm, he was the one chosen to design Global Oil's Tulsa headquarters. If that didn't guarantee his name would be next, nothing would.

"I think that's a way of carrying on the legacy," Ted added for emphasis.

Or was it really?

As he turned around, Wyatt had the audacity to laugh. "So becoming a big-shot architect is more important than doing what you really want?"

This should be interesting. Ted crossed both arms over his chest. "What is it you think I really want to do?"

"Don't you think I've seen how you look at the old cabin over there ever since you left off playing football? And I know you can't walk down Main Street in town without trying to figure out how to fix up every old building there. That's how you've been since we were kids. Oh, and forget about your phone conversations with Pop. That's all the two of you talk about."

Much as he hated to admit it, his brother spoke the truth. "What's your point?"

Wyatt stared him straight in the eyes, his expression daring Ted to disagree. "The point is, even though you live a fancy life in the big city, I think you want to be me."

Ted forced a laugh. "Is that the best you can do?"

"Is that the best *you* can do, Ted?"

Several arguments came to mind. None applied, however.

His younger brother shook his head. "I'm right. Admit

it." Wyatt continued without waiting for Ted to respond. "If you're excited by all this old stuff, why don't you put your money where your mouth is and do something about those old buildings downtown?"

This time Ted's laughter came quickly and without effort. "Oh, sure, it's just that easy."

"Go ahead and laugh, but I was talking to Bob Tratelli and Landon Gallier the other day, and they said the mayor's bound and determined to tear them all down and put up some kind of fancy outlet mall. Something about modernizing Latagnier being his legacy." He paused. "Bob said he's been trying to buy up some of these places, but most of them aren't meeting code, so it doesn't matter who owns them. Once they're condemned, they're going down. You know what that means, don't you?"

When Ted said nothing, Wyatt gave him a look and stormed off. Ted caught up with Wyatt on the porch. The need to argue pressed hard, but the truth prevailed. "Yeah, I know what it means. And for the record, I've been talking to Bob, too. Giving him some advice is all." He paused. "So maybe I do want to be you," he said as he gave his brother a playful jab in the ribs. "Who wouldn't want to be young and dumb? It makes the world much less complicated."

"Young and dumb, huh?" Wyatt returned the jab. "Sure beats old and slow, but then, I always was able to beat you in a race to the bayou."

"Is that so?" With that taunt, the race was on.

By the time he reached the bayou, Ted cared less about who won and more about finding a soft place to fall down and gasp for breath. How long had it been since he'd made the run to the bayou? Obviously too long.

"I'd blame city life," Wyatt said as he plopped down beside Ted, barely winded.

Ted leaned back against the soft grass and ignored his

brother in favor of watching a fat white cloud drift by. Thoughts of tomorrow and the partners' meeting at the firm began to intrude, ruining the moment. Still, he allowed them.

It was what he wanted, wasn't it? This life, he'd chosen it.

Or had he allowed it to choose him?

Football—now that had been a career he'd loved and hated all at the same time. While he'd disliked the toll it took on his body, Ted was hard-pressed to find anything that beat the thrill of running for a touchdown or winning a particularly hard-fought game.

One thing he never second-guessed was his early retirement from the sport. Leaving the game at the top of his career was the best choice he'd made. Indeed, the Lord had led him away before his collection of scars and aches had grown to be something other than mere irritations.

As God always did, He led Ted to the next best thing besides a touchdown: a career in which he could exercise his love for architectural treasures with the same measure of excitement he once gave to football alone. Truthfully, he found more fun in the challenge of dusting off an old building and bringing it back to its former glory than in the championship ring gathering dust in his safe-deposit box at the bank in Baton Rouge.

And yet you're about to sign on as chief architect on a Tulsa high-rise project. A modern skyscraper without any redeeming historical value other than the fact it's likely to cause a number of grand old homes near downtown to be razed.

When he thought of it that way, the choice made no sense.

Gradually, his breathing slowed, and he rolled onto his side. "You were right," he said, surprising himself as the words escaped. "I do wish I were you."

"So you said." Wyatt snapped off a blade of grass and began to fashion a whistle. "And yet I'd trade you that old house back there for your slick bachelor pad in a heartbeat."

All Ted could manage was a snort that his mama would have swatted him for. There was more love and life in the structure Wyatt called "that old house" than his "slick bachelor pad" would ever see.

At least as long as Ted lived there, anyway.

Wyatt met Ted's gaze. "So what? You'll live in Baton Rouge and make your next million in a year or two, and I'll still be in Latagnier coaching high school football and teaching computer classes to teenagers who would rather be anywhere but in class."

"What would you do if you weren't teaching, Wyatt?" Ted rose up on his elbow and smiled. "If you got that chance to swap lives."

"Not lives," he corrected. "Just homes. And the answer is easy. I'd quit teaching in a New York minute and take that IT job Ernest keeps offering to me up in Baton Rouge."

At the mention of their cousin, owner of a company that specialized in oil-exploration software, Ted sat up and swiped at the pieces of grass on his elbow. "I didn't realize you were interested in that kind of work." He paused, the picture suddenly clear. "Hey, you stuck around so someone would be living in the house, didn't you?" He gave Wyatt a nudge. "That's it, isn't it?"

Wyatt blew on the blade of grass, making a shrill sound. A moment later he cast the blade away and turned his attention to Ted. "Someone had to keep it from falling down, Ted. And, yeah, I know I could have called Pop back home to run the place, but I didn't have the heart to. Building those churches is the only thing that's put a sparkle in his eyes since Mom died."

"Yeah," Ted said as he climbed to his feet then offered his hand to help Wyatt up. "I had no idea you had any ambition to do anything more than teach."

The wounded look in his brother's eyes made Ted cringe.

Before he could apologize, Wyatt clamped a hand onto his shoulder. "You didn't know because I never told you." He paused. "I also never told you how much I appreciated the times you've come to my rescue."

"Hey, we're family," Ted said as lightly as he could, "and that's what family does."

"I suppose, but I never intended to call on you like I have. It's just that this place takes the kind of upkeep I can't seem to manage. I hated to admit that there were times when I had to pay people to fix a roof or patch up plumbing, because I knew how that would look to you and Pop." He paused. "I'm a computer guy, Ted. Home repair is not what I do best."

Ted shook his head. "What're you talking about?"

Wyatt shrugged. "I'm a Breaux. We're supposed to be carpenters. Our relatives built this town, and you build entire buildings, for crying out loud. I just felt a little, well, stupid at not being able to do what our dad or his dad could do." He met Ted's gaze. "So instead of calling Pop to come and fix whatever was broken, I ran up bills a high school computer teacher's salary couldn't pay. The irony is, if I'd taken the IT job, I could have paid for the work two or three times over, but then who would be here seeing to this place?"

Speechless, Ted could only look away. For a moment, he studied the dark water of the bayou. His image of Wyatt had been all wrong, something he'd need to contemplate a bit. Finally, he cleared his throat and braved a glance at Wyatt. "I never knew you bankrupted yourself keeping this place up. I thought it must have been. . .well. . .something else."

His brother met his stare head-on. "You never asked."

The truth of that statement stung. "No, I didn't." Ted shrugged. "But I should've. It won't happen again."

"Nothing you can do about it now. The past is the past." Then Wyatt was off, striding ahead to turn away from the bayou and toward the house. Ted followed a step behind.

Or was the past his future? He stopped short and turned back to face the bayou. From somewhere deep inside, he felt something stir. A hope—no, a dream—that promised to rise to the surface should he allow it.

Dare he? Ted squared his shoulders. In all his years playing football, he'd never felt fear, only exhilaration and cautious optimism when faced with a charging opponent. Somehow the idea now stirring about in his addled brain struck terror into him like nothing he'd ever felt.

But it also made him smile.

"Hey, old dude," Wyatt called. "In case you're lost, the house is over here. It's the big wooden thing with the cable dish you complain 'ruins the line of the roof.'"

Ted began to laugh at his brother's dead-on impression and found he couldn't stop. His strength suddenly renewed, he jogged toward Wyatt then picked up speed and raced past him. With each step, the load that had been riding on his shoulders seemed lighter, and his purpose looked clearer. *Lord, if You're not behind this, stop me, but if You're for it, show me how You want it to happen.*

Wyatt loped up beside him. "What's going on with you?"

Barely slowing his speed, Ted yanked his phone from his pocket and punched in the number for his old friend Bob Tratelli. Next he would hunt up Landon Gallier and test the idea on him.

It's now or never, he thought as Bob's phone began to ring. If he didn't act before good sense prevailed, he might never again find the courage.

two

Houston, Texas, one year later

Days like today made Lise Gentry hate the fact that she was the baby of the family. No one ever took her seriously.

Ever.

When she said she wanted a set of building blocks, her parents insisted on baby dolls. Her proposal to forgo a trip to summer camp in favor of a mission trip to build houses was also ignored. The last straw came when her requested high school graduation gift of a table saw was bypassed in favor of a pearl necklace and matching bracelet. If only she'd had the gumption to pawn the baubles. At least she'd found the courage to change her major to architecture after spending two full semesters barely passing the classes that would have sent her down her mother's preferred path of teaching.

Then there was the fact that her choice of architecture led her to Houston and a career with Restoration Associates, an up-and-coming firm determined to change the world one crumbling downtown at a time. While she learned her craft from Ryan Jennings, one of the premier architects in the field of urban renewal, she also fell in love—with Ryan, a confirmed bachelor. Mother pronounced it all most improper.

Lise sighed. That was a time when she'd been the one not listening.

All of this Lise recalled as she endured her sister, Susan, talking at length about napkin folding. Finally, Susan took a breath, and Lise seized her opportunity. "Why don't you e-mail me about this, and I'll check it out when I get to the site."

"Hey. You're going out of town, aren't you? Do you have any idea what you're doing? The party is *imminent*."

Imminent. Susan always did have a flair for the dramatic. If only Mother hadn't deemed theater an unsuitable profession for a lady. Unfortunately, that left those in Susan's path forever paying for the absence of an outlet for her directorial talents.

"Of course I know what I'm doing. And the party is not *imminent*. At best, it's upcoming. On the horizon, perhaps. But definitely not *imminent*."

Silence.

Great. Now she'd done it. Well, at least Susan had finally listened. Lise supported the cell phone between her ear and shoulder as she closed her suitcase. "I'm set to return in a week, Susan. Ten days at the most. I'll be back in plenty of time for the party."

"This is not just any party, Annalise Gentry," her older sister said sharply. "It's their *fortieth* anniversary."

How well she knew. Away from the presence of their older sister, Lise and her brother, Troy, had taken to calling the ever-growing extravaganza the party of the decade, or POD for short. What Susan would do on the occasion of their parents' fiftieth anniversary also gave much cause for speculation. "And this is not a vacation, Susan; it's a business trip. The downtown rehab, remember?"

"Rehab?" Her sister paused. "No, I don't recall—"

"The downtown rehab." Lise let out a long breath and moderated her voice. "It's my first big redesign without having to report to. . ." She paused, reluctant to mention Ryan's name to her sister. "I'm going to save a downtown and pay my mortgage for another year. It's kind of a big deal, actually."

Susan chuckled, but there was no humor in the sound. "I thought that was just something that *might* happen, unlike our parents' anniversary party, which *will* happen whether you are part of it or not."

Truth be told, she didn't have the job yet, but she would. Awarding the project to Restoration Associates was merely a formality. At least that's what Ryan had been told by the mayor, a stout man with an interesting accent and, according to her boss, a fondness for a good steak. Her only competition was a local fellow.

"Hardly any competition for Restoration Associates," Ryan had pronounced.

"Look," Lise said gently, "in order to hold up my end of the financial bargain, I must work. Besides, I'm sure you've got it all under control. Tell me again about the place you found to hold the ceremony."

"You're stalling."

"I'm interested."

Lise hefted the suitcase off the bed and set it on the floor then caught the phone just before it slipped out of her reach. Of course, her sister hadn't noticed her absence.

But then, Susan wouldn't—not when she was in one of her moods. One of the twins must be teething.

"Look, honey, I love you, but I must go," Lise said. "If you need me, I'll be in Latagnier. It's not like I'm on the other side of the world."

"No, that's true, but some days I think it's easier to get in touch with Troy out on the mission field in Ecuador than to have a decent conversation with you." She paused, and Lise waited for what she knew was coming. "Lise, you work too much. Have you given any thought to settling down? Allowing a new man in your life would certainly not be the end of the world."

Lise cast a glance around her nearly empty bedroom then yanked the suitcase into an upright position and rolled it into the hall. "Susan, my life is plenty full without adding any complications to it."

"I'm not suggesting a complication," she said in that voice that sounded eerily similar to Mom's. "I know your heart's still healing from that awful man's betrayal."

That awful man. Ryan had been anything but awful, although Susan was right about the betrayal. Seven months and counting, and she'd not yet managed to shake it. Of course, it would help if she changed jobs, but that wasn't about to happen right now. Losing your heart to your boss was one thing, but losing the best job you'd ever had because the boss broke your heart was another thing altogether.

Thankfully, the job in Latagnier would keep her away from Houston and Ryan for months.

She parked the suitcase by the front door then reached for her purse and briefcase. With any luck, she'd be out of the house and this conversation in short order. To that end, she began her search for her keys.

"What I'm saying," Susan continued as Lise upended a sofa cushion, "is to go find yourself a middleman."

She set the cushion straight then spied her keys peeking from beneath the rug. How things went missing in her life was a perpetual mystery.

"Lise, did you hear me?"

Palming her keys, Lise strode to the front door, glancing at her watch as she sidestepped a sofa pillow. "Hmm? What? I'm sorry."

"I said," Susan drawled in her I-am-exasperated-and-I-want-you-to know-it tone, "you need a middleman. Of course, he will have to see beyond frumpy to the beautiful woman you are. For once in your life, Lise, do something audacious, won't you?"

Frumpy? Lise looked down at her perfectly matched ensemble and frowned. What was wrong with plaid Bermuda shorts and a polo shirt the color of her tan sneakers?

"Are you ignoring me, Lise?"

As if that were even remotely possible.

"I'm audacious," she said in meek defense.

"All right," Susan said slowly. "Tell me the last audacious thing you did."

"Fine." Lise sighed as she stepped outside. "A middleman and a makeover it is. Set me up for one of each while you're out shopping today, but remember I won't be back until the Friday after Labor Day weekend. Now, I love you, but I must go."

Lise tucked her phone into her purse and locked the door then made a mad dash for her car through the raindrops. Suddenly, the appeal of living in her architecturally significant late-nineteenth-century cottage in Garden Oaks did not make up for the fact that the garage was not large enough to accommodate her twenty-first-century sport-utility vehicle. Somehow she managed to stuff her bag in the back and start the engine before the rain drenched her.

Then the phone rang. Snapping her seat belt, she glanced down at the screen.

Of course. Susan.

Debating whether to answer the phone did no good. As the eldest sibling, Susan had long ago decided that a phone call from her took precedence over anything and everything. In short, she would call until the phone was answered, and no excuse would suffice.

Lise turned her wipers on and settled the hands-free device over her ear then pushed the button. "Hello, Susan. What can I do for you now?"

"Sarcasm does not a lady make."

"Susan," she said as she signaled to turn onto Garden Oaks Boulevard, "has anyone ever told you that you sound just like Mom?"

"I'm going to ignore the fact that you likely did not intend that as a compliment. Look, this thing with Ryan was over before it began. It just took you six months—"

"Seven," Lise interrupted.

"All right. *Seven* months," Susan continued, "to realize it."

Lise ignored the pause in her sister's speech. Likely Susan wanted a confirmation that she was over Ryan, and that was something she could not say with any assurance.

Over the *thought* of Ryan, yes. Over what Ryan's abrupt ending of their personal relationship had done to her?

No way.

"I've only got a few minutes before the girls wake up from their naps, and I'm sure you're not sorry to hear that, Lise. You always get so defensive when I try to talk to you about men. It's just that. . ." Her sister's voice softened. "Well, you've got so much to offer that special someone. I'm so sorry it wasn't Ryan. At least he's smart enough to recognize the fact that you're the best architect he's ever hired. I have to give him credit for that."

Tears began to well in Lise's eyes, mirroring the drops splattering her windshield. An answer eluded her, so she settled for biting her lip and focusing on the road.

"So back to the middleman theory." Susan's tone brightened. "Here's the thing. Sometimes God's timing isn't the same as ours. I think sometimes He allows for that by letting us find that middleman in between the guy who broke our heart and the one He intends for us to spend our life with. The middleman is the guy who unbreaks our heart but doesn't stick around to capture it forever."

"Interesting theology, Suse." The light ahead turned red, and Lise rolled her car to a stop then reached into the console for a tissue. "So you're saying I should find a middleman to fix my heart?"

"Well, technically only the Lord can take care of your heart, but I think that's exactly what you need. Just remember the most important part: Never marry the middleman."

Lise managed a smile. No danger of that.

No, she intended to take this job and do the firm proud.

Inside her briefcase were not only the blueprints to a renovation project but also a plan to cure the blues she'd carried with her since Ryan decided to step out.

Indeed, the project in downtown Latagnier, Louisiana, would do more than make the town sparkle. It would be a new and fresh start to a life that did not include an attachment to any man—not even a middleman.

three

Latagnier, Louisiana

Ted Breaux stood at the old casement window and stared down at the city of Latagnier two floors below. The original glass made for a slightly skewed view, but only a few would trade clear vision for the rippled and flawed panes.

He ran a hand over the wooden mullion and smiled. It was hard to believe barely a year had passed since the conversation with his brother that changed his life.

In the twelve months since he'd handed his condo over to Wyatt and moved home to Latagnier, much had happened. His mother always said God tended to work in "suddenlys" when doing something big. That had certainly been the case for Ted. Little time passed between the day he gave his two weeks' notice and the day BTG Holdings was born over a cup of coffee at the Java Hut in downtown Latagnier.

The corporation formed by Ted, Bob Tratelli, and Landon Gallier had become quite well known for purchasing and restoring Latagnier's landmark buildings. Theirs was a partnership that worked well. While Ted acted as architect and designer for the projects, Landon was the on-site construction manager and general go-to guy. Busy running Tratelli Aviation, Bob preferred to take a less active role, although he never missed a board meeting and never failed to have an opinion on whatever the issue of the moment might be. He also handled the books, which gave Ted and Landon the time to do what they did best.

To date, they'd bought and repurposed two structures on

the city's list of potential teardowns: the ice cream parlor and the building where Ted stood. Just yesterday he'd finished the plans for updating the Bayou Place Hotel down the block, a project Landon would take on next week. Ted had plans to add the old mercantile to their list of properties, and he'd decided to purchase his late grandmother's house near the post office.

The former, once restored, would make a fine office building for the oil-related companies that were now following the trend to move their personnel closer to the fields. The latter, a sentimental purchase, would need a little work but would hold great value in his heart.

Ted frowned and took a step away from the window. Pop had been holding those properties for ages. The likelihood that he would sell was low, but Ted had begun praying for direction in that area. With his father busy building churches and burning up the miles in his RV, perhaps now was the time to begin pressing him to sell. Maintaining the family-owned sites had become quite a chore, one Pop was rarely around to accomplish anymore.

Thankfully, the mercantile still stood sound and without many safety concerns. Granny's house, however, was another matter. Until recently, it was empty and a ripe target for vandals or burglars. Now that it was ready to be rented, the only concern was keeping the place in fit condition for the future tenant, whomever that would be. At least Pop had been able to find someone to take care of the flower beds and keep the grass cut.

Ted sighed. He wasn't too old to remember the days when the citizens of Latagnier believed a locked door was unnecessary.

His gaze fell on the roof of the hardware store in the next block. Memories of trips to town with his grandfather brought a smile to his face. While Wyatt tagged along with their grandmother to the mercantile in the hopes of first

pick of whatever treat she would buy them, Ted never failed
to follow a step behind Granddad as they slowly made their
way down aisles filled with every sort of tool and trim.

It was where his love of carpentry, born at his father's and
grandfather's knees, was nurtured. The day it closed was the
day he vowed to see that a tragedy of that sort never again
happened to Latagnier.

How far he'd come since then. And yet there was still
so much left to do. If only he'd been able to purchase the
hardware building when the Collier heirs put it up for sale.
Some conglomerate out of Kansas City had outbid BTG by a
substantial amount, leaving Ted to worry about the building's
future.

He leaned forward to get a better look at the building's
facade. If he squinted, he could still see some of the letters
spelling out LATAGNIER HARDWARE AND BUILDING SUPPLY
that had been last touched up sometime during the Depression.
Only the cornerstone, with its boldly carved date of 1893, could
still be easily read.

"Surely the suits who own the place can see the value in it,"
he muttered.

The phone rang in the outer office, and Ted waited to hear
whether the caller was phoning for him or Landon. "Mr.
Tratelli on line two, sir," his secretary called.

"Thanks, Bea." Ted shook his head. Never one to stand on
formality, the spry senior citizen had long since abandoned
the state-of-the-art communications system in favor of
shouting the name of whomever she needed.

He picked up the phone and eased into his chair. "*Comment
ça va,* Bob?"

"*Ça va bien,* kid."

He chuckled. It seemed as though Bob took every opportunity to remind Ted of the fact that he, of the three, was the
youngest by half a decade.

Ted flexed the knee that had plagued him the last half of his NFL career and grimaced. "If you could hear how I'm creaking and groaning today, you'd be calling me 'old man' instead of 'kid.'"

"You haven't been falling through stairs again, have you?"

"Nah," Ted said. "I've learned my lesson. Next time I'm questioning the stability of something, I'll send Landon in. He's smaller and faster than I am."

"Seriously," Bob said, "you need to stop taking chances. I know you love these old buildings, but you can't tromp around in them like there's no possibility of getting hurt. Promise me you'll be more careful. It's not likely we'll get this contract if our architect is out of commission."

"Hey, I'm a Breaux and so was your mother. Who knows? The way things work around here, Landon's probably some distant cousin of ours. This town was practically built with Breaux hands. How can anyone possibly think anyone but a Breaux could rebuild it?"

"Be that as it may, I still want you to be careful. Have you spoken to Landon about a safety meeting for the new crew? I know the hotel's going to be a bigger project than the others we've tackled, and I don't want to hear that some poor guy messed up a knee falling through rotting floorboards." He paused. "Or a crumbling staircase."

"Who are we talking about now? Me or the crew?"

"Well, now that you mention it. . ."

Bob's safety chats were legendary, likely a result of his short stint as a stuntman in his grandfather's movies. Ted glanced at the clock. A quarter to ten and he'd accomplished nothing more than consuming two cups of coffee and reading his e-mails.

Time to change the subject. "So we still on for lunch?"

"Yeah, I've been meaning to talk to you about that." Bob paused. "I've been praying about something, and I'd like to run it past you."

Bea strolled in and tossed a package atop the teetering pile on the corner of Ted's desk then added a fresh cup of coffee to the clutter beside his computer. Before he could thank her, his secretary was gone.

Ted reached for the steaming mug. "Sure, what's that?"

"I don't know if I've told you how much I appreciate the accountability of meeting with you every week. I know it's helped me to realize how important it is to go through life with someone who's got your back but also isn't afraid to tell you when you're about to mess up."

"Ditto."

And he meant it. Without their weekly accountability meetings, first begun by phone then changed to in-person conversations over coffee, lunch, or, on rare occasions, dinner, there was no telling where Ted would be. BTG Holdings would certainly only be a good idea, and moving to Latagnier would still be a dream.

"Well, anyway." Another pause. "I had this idea."

"So you said." Ted set the mug down. This must be big; else the straight-shooting Tratelli would've blurted it out long before now. "Spit it out, Bob. You've got me concerned here."

"It's just that, well, I'm a little hesitant to make any changes since it's working so well, but, well, I wondered if we might consider letting another member into the meetings."

"Another member?"

"Yeah. Landon's got some. . .well. . .he could use prayer." Another pause. "And accountability."

He jerked to attention. "He's not drinking again, is he?"

"No," Bob said quickly, "and I'd like to keep it that way. More important, I think he would, too. So what do you think? Do we have room for one more on the team?"

Ted swiveled his chair toward the window and watched the afternoon breeze toss the limbs of a stand of pines in the distance. "Yeah," he said slowly, "I believe we do."

❧

Landon Gallier sipped at his coffee like a man intent on thinking over just the right words. Ted watched him, waiting to see if the man they'd let into their weekly meetings would admit to what was bothering him.

Around them, the lunch crowd at the City Grill had begun to trickle out, leaving only the most leisurely of diners in their black vinyl booths. Ted folded his napkin and set it over the remains of his lunch then took a long drink of sweet tea as the waitress swept his plate away.

"So," Bob said, "I told Bliss I'd just let her do whatever she wanted about the cake shop, although I have to admit I'm wishing she didn't work so hard. I'd rather know she was home taking it easy."

Ted turned his attention to Bob. "She probably thinks the same about you."

His friend ducked his head in mock dismay. Bob's schedule was an ongoing prayer issue. "Ouch."

Looking to Landon, Ted waited a moment to see if he might join the conversation. He'd found during their lunch that Landon was quick to talk about almost anything but himself. Even reminiscing about his glory days as the high school quarterback didn't bring much in the way of discussion.

It appeared iffy as to whether the group would remain a trio after today. From the beginning, the rule had always been full disclosure and complete honesty. With the check now sitting on the table and lunch nearing its end, Landon Gallier remained as closemouthed as ever.

"So, Landon," Ted said, "any advice or questions for Bob? Just so you know, Bliss isn't thrilled with the fact that he's married to her and his job."

"It's not all that bad," Bob argued. "I'm getting a lot better."

"What about the twins?" Landon said. "With Bliss's mother working as your secretary, who keeps them? You're not worried she's spending too much time away from them, are you?"

"She rarely lets them out of her sight unless my mom or hers is around to watch them." Bob shook his head. "I don't know how she does it, but the woman somehow manages to run that cake shop and chase a pair of three-year-olds around without breaking a sweat."

"She's a woman," Landon said, his expression tight and guarded. "They're tougher than us. I think God must have made 'em that way."

"I suppose so." Bob met Ted's gaze as if prompting him to guide the conversation elsewhere.

"Yeah, well," Ted began, "I don't know much about women beyond the fact that until a man marries, he somehow manages to fend for himself just fine. Once the preacher pronounces the 'I dos,' suddenly a man becomes this person who can't even pick out his own socks."

"Hey, I resemble that," Bob said with a laugh. "Besides, who needs to make decisions when you have a wife to do it for you? I say it makes the day a whole lot less complicated. What about you, Landon?"

The construction foreman thought about the question a moment too long, prompting Ted to jump in. "Yeah, well, I figure I'm doing just fine on my own. I'll stick to watching the two of you lose the ability to dress yourselves or make a sandwich without calling on the little woman for help."

Bob grinned, but Landon still seemed to be stuck on the previous question. "You okay, Gallier?" Bob finally asked.

"Okay? Yeah, I guess I am." Landon shrugged and reached for his wallet. "So is this what the two of you do every week? Debate the great question of whether a man is better off married or single?"

"Of course not. What would be the point? I know I'm right and so does Bob. For him, being married is a good thing. For me, being single is, well, better than a good thing."

Bob chuckled, and slowly so did Landon. The tension diffused momentarily. As the waitress filled his tea glass, Ted leaned back against the cracked vinyl of the booth and bit his tongue until he could no longer keep silent. Finally, Ted leveled a hard look at Landon. "So, bottom line. Are you drinking again?"

Landon slapped a ten-dollar bill on top of the check and rose. "Thanks for the invite to lunch. I've got work to get back to. I'll leave you to your confession session."

"Coward."

The word slipped from Ted's mouth before he had time to think. Hanging between them, the accusation seemed to take its time sinking in. In slow measures, however, Landon crumpled back onto the bench. When he looked up, his stare held no more defiance, only defeat.

"Yeah," Landon finally said, "that's exactly what I am. A coward. I know the right things to do, and yet I just go my own way and do what I shouldn't."

Silence reigned at the table while around them silverware clanged against chipped bone china and feet scuffled across old wooden floors. Somewhere in the depths of the kitchen, the fry cook called an order number. Still, at table number 5, no one spoke.

Then Ted found his voice. "Yeah, me, too, Landon," he said. "Without Bob to keep me accountable, I'd be the same old man I always was. Bullheaded, stubborn, hard to please, and more than a little irritating. Oh, and did I mention I was a perfectionist who never did like to listen to anyone else's opinions but my own?"

"You still are," Bob teased. "Thank goodness I'm perfect, or we'd really have a problem."

The aviator's quip worked its magic, and the tension eased. While Bob continued to expound on his perfection, Landon jumped in with a few comments on the error of his theory. Somewhere along the way, the check was paid and the table cleared. Conversation drifted back toward work and the upcoming renovations at the Bayou Place Hotel.

Finally, Bob checked his watch. "I believe I'll take advantage of the beautiful weather and take my wife up for a spin in the Piper; that is, if she can be persuaded to leave the cake shop. I know for a fact my parents have the kids until suppertime."

"I've never understood why you take her up in that plane," Landon said. "My Neecie wouldn't fly in an open cockpit if you paid her. It might mess up her hair."

"That plane and I go way back. She was my dad's, you know, so flying her might be a little uncomfortable compared to other planes, but it does take me back." Bob smiled. "I'll admit I might enjoy the flights a little more than she does, but my Bliss is a trouper."

Ted listened as the men jabbered on about their wives as long as he could stand it. Finally, he set his hands on the table and exhaled long and hard.

"Okay, so I'll go back and take another look at the plans for the downtown project," Ted said. "I know that outfit out of Texas doesn't stand a chance against us, but I still intend to go into the meeting on Tuesday with a fully developed plan and an answer for anything the mayor throws at me. You know he's still irritated with me for fighting him on the demolition of the hardware store."

"It was the right thing to do," Bob said. "The old place might not be as pretty as she once was, but under all that crumbling brick and peeling paint are a whole lot of good memories and strong timber."

"That's the truth," Ted agreed. "I just wish we could've got our hands on her. Of course, the Kansas boys might get tired of holding on to it and be persuaded to sell."

Bob nodded. "With the profits we're going to make from the downtown renovation, I'd say we can safely offer them a good price."

Ted smiled. "Another reason to be sure I've got all my details down. I'm sure Harlon Dorsey would love nothing better than to see me make a fool out of myself."

"At this point, you probably dream about that job." Landon pushed away from the table but made no move to stand. "Why ruin it with overkill? Just go in and tell them what you know. It'll be fine. Harlon can be a bag of wind when he wants to be, but deep down he knows he's got the people of Latagnier to answer to."

"True," Ted said.

"Of course it is. Now I'm going to leave you office types and get back to work. In the meantime, stay out of my job sites until I declare the stairs are fit to walk on. Last thing I need is to lose a tenderfoot on a construction site. Remember, I'm the quarterback on that field and you're the receiver. I call the plays, get it?"

He made the last statement with a hint of a smile. A moment later, however, Landon grew serious again. "About this weekly thing."

"Yeah?" Bob said. "What about it?"

The former quarterback studied the keys in his palm. "I think I'll be back next week, if that's all right with you two."

four

On Interstate 10 between Houston and Latagnier

Thoughts of the project carried Lise halfway through the nearly five-hour drive to tiny Latagnier. Somewhere between Beaumont and Lake Charles, the sun had come out. On a whim, she stopped at a tourist trap near a city called Iowa—oddly pronounced I-O-Way—and bought the most audacious pair of sunglasses she could find. They were white with a smattering of rhinestones that sparkled in the afternoon sun.

At the next exit, she found an outlet mall and exchanged her Bermuda shorts and khaki polo shirt for a cute sundress in sunshine yellow. As an afterthought, she threw a pair of white sandals from the 3/$10 rack into her cart. They were a half size too big and only stayed on when she shuffled her feet, but they were the total opposite of every piece of footwear in her closet back in Houston.

Now let Susan call her frumpy.

Her mission complete, the new and improved Lise returned to the dark ribbon of highway that led to Latagnier, Louisiana. If her middleman happened to be waiting there, he would now have less trouble finding her.

Finding the Depression-era Bayou Place Hotel was a simple matter and locating a parking spot simpler still. It seemed as though she might be the only guest tonight, a fact borne out by the empty lobby and eagerly attentive staff. Before she could finish saying her name, a bellman had saluted smartly and slung her bag over his shoulder. In the process, he bypassed a

31

perfectly good but definitely antiquated luggage cart parked beside a staircase that looked, except for the beige industrial-grade carpet, as if it had come straight out of the closing scene of *Gone with the Wind*. Unfortunately, the rest of the space looked much less grand.

In fact, from the looks of the Bayou Place lobby, things had changed little in the old hotel since the original designers completed the project. As she shuffled toward the reception desk, Lise made a mental note to send a memo about adding this property to the list of buildings being restored.

The gray-haired woman on the other side of the counter looked up with a smile. "*Bienvenue!* You must be Miss Gentry."

"Yes, I am," she said as she watched the porter disappear behind the overlarge palm tree that provided the only color in an otherwise overwhelmingly beige room. "Sir," she called. "Excuse me. Where are you going with my bag? I haven't got my—"

A tug at her sleeve made Lise turn around. The woman held an old-fashioned key tied with a scarlet cord. At the end of the cord was something that looked like a price tag at a yard sale. The number 1 had been emblazoned on both sides along with the warning PROPERTY OF BAYOU PLACE HOTEL. DO NOT TAKE THIS HOME WITH YOU.

Lise peered down at the key, now pressed into her palm, then glanced up at the woman's name tag. "Thank you, Gertrude. I take it I'm in room 1."

"You are. Turn right at the top of the stairs," she said. "And it's Gert."

She scanned the lobby for the elevator then glanced over her shoulder at Gert, who was busy picking lint off the sleeve of her dark green blazer. "Guess I'm going to get my exercise while I'm here," she said under her breath as she shouldered her briefcase and set out up the wide carpeted staircase.

"You need a wake-up call, hon?"

Lise smiled over her shoulder. "Yes, please. Six thirty."

"Six thirty it is." Gert reached for a pen. "You need room service, too?"

"No, thank you," she said. "I thought I might go out for dinner. Can you recommend a place near the hotel?"

For a moment, Gert seemed deep in thought. "Well, there's the Java Hut, but they've only got coffee. There's the Dip Cone, but I don't reckon you're the type who'd call ice cream a proper supper."

"Not really." Lise shrugged. "Maybe I'll just take a look at the phone book and see what appeals." Giving up on any pretense, she slipped off her sandals and marched up the stairs with her most regal posture.

"Suit yourself," Gert called as Lise reached the top of the stairs and spied the door to room 1.

Fortunately, the room was a bit less bland than the all-beige lobby. Unfortunately, the riot of colors began at her toes with a rose-patterned carpet and ended at the opposite wall where a pair of heavy red drapes with matching tasseled trim obliterated any chance of seeing the sunshine outside. Somehow her bag had preceded her and now sat at the foot of a bed clad in garish green sprigged with a random pattern of tiny red roses. Had she been prone to vertigo, the room might have sent her spinning. Rather, she set her briefcase on the art deco mirrored desk, dropped her sandals on the carpet, and fell onto the bed. Her stomach complained, but she ignored it. A short nap and she'd be ready to tackle finding a decent meal.

Or maybe she'd just make a stop at the Dip Cone.

The phone rang, jarring her from a dreamless sleep. "Did you mean 6:30 a.m. or 6:30 p.m., hon?"

Lise stretched and cleared her throat. "A.m., please," she managed.

"A.m. it is," Gert said then hung up.

Now wide-awake and hungrier than ever, Lise rose and stretched then spied her reflection in the mirror—and in the desk. Even with the wrinkles in her dress and the red marks from where the ruffles on the pillows had creased her cheeks, she looked anything but frumpy.

In fact, she looked downright audacious.

With that knowledge, Lise grabbed her sunglasses and slipped into her sandals to head downstairs. The newly audacious Lise found the Dip Cone with no problem. Of course, being the only establishment open this close to dark made the job an easy one.

She opened the door and walked into the 1950s. The shop wore the same color of red as the guest room's curtains on its long, narrow walls, and the floor sported black-and-white linoleum that likely predated the invention of air-conditioning. As the door shut behind her, a bell jangled. She half expected to see some fifties-clad fellow complete with cap and bow tie at the cash register awaiting her order with a grin, but that's where the authenticity stopped.

Rather, the twenty-first-century teen behind the counter seemed to have little interest in doing anything except making the pair of blond cheerleader types at the cash register giggle. When the girls finally moved toward the door and escaped into the heat, the kid turned his less-than-thrilled countenance on Lise.

"Yeah?" It was a word, a question, and a comment on how little he appreciated the interruption all rolled into one syllable.

The array of choices bedazzled her, and for a moment Lise could only stand transfixed. The old Lise would order vanilla or, on a daring day, vanilla bean. "I've never had boysenberry ice cream." She lifted her gaze to the youth. "Is it any good?"

The clanging of the bell on the door interrupted a grunt

that seemed to indicate he had no opinion. Out of the corner of her eye, she saw a man approach. Great. Now she had to decide.

"One scoop double dark chocolate caramel, please," she said.

"Any mix-ins?" The kid's dark brow lifted as if to dare her to take her time answering.

Again Lise perused the choices. Everything from pieces of peanut butter to scoops of breakfast cereal beckoned. She eyed the chopped-up candy bar, and her stomach growled in protest. What would the new and improved Lise get? She looked down at her sandals and contemplated the question.

"Is that a no?" Said without a single inflection.

She looked up at the kid. Obviously, he wouldn't know audacious from awful.

The fellow who'd been waiting behind her stepped into Lise's line of vision. "I recommend the red hots. You wouldn't think so, but they're amazing with double dark chocolate caramel."

Lise looked up into eyes that rivaled the color of the ice cream she'd just chosen and forced a smile. A second later, she did the customary left-hand ring check and found the coast clear.

Well, hello. You must be the first candidate in my unofficial search for the middleman.

"Then I guess I ought to try it," she said. "If you recommend it, that is."

"Oh, I recommend it highly. Around here the only thing better than double dark chocolate caramel with red hots is a big ole pot of shrimp gumbo."

Again her stomach growled. "Sounds wonderful."

"It was. Unfortunately, the best place to eat gumbo was just closed to make room for some chain store." The corners of the chocolate eyes crinkled as he smiled. "But that's another story for another day." He addressed the kid. "One for me, too, Andrew. And this time don't short me on the mix-ins or I'll tell your dad."

Andrew gave him a look that was surprisingly less hostile. "Tell him when you see him tomorrow, Uncle Ted."

Despite his claim, the kid poured in an ample amount of the spicy candies. In short order, he'd stabbed, mixed, and stirred the mixture until an oversized scoop of ice cream sat on each of the cones.

"Four sixty," he said.

Lise reached for her purse and realized she'd left it in her room. "Oh no," she said. "I'm sorry, but I can't pay for that. My money's back at the hotel."

She turned to head for the door, but the brown-eyed man stopped her. "My treat," Uncle Ted said as he offered her the larger of the cones.

"I really couldn't," she said as she attempted to remove her attention from the cleft in his chin and the dimple that dotted his left cheek. "Unless I was to pay you back, of course."

"Of course," he said. "Now what say we go find a place to sit and enjoy these before they melt?"

He looked honest enough, and it didn't hurt that he was quite handsome. Plus, they were in a public place. And he *was* Andrew's uncle.

"Why not?" Lise followed the man's broad back to the nearest booth then slid in across from him. Perhaps a bit of audaciousness was in order. "So," she said as she wrapped a napkin around the bottom of the cone, "you come here often?"

The fellow's laughter was deep and quick. "You're funny," he said. "And obviously not from around here."

Out of words, she took a bite of the concoction and pronounced it heavenly. He gave her a look that said, "I told you so."

"So," she said, emboldened, "how do you know I'm not from around here?"

Uncle Ted dabbed at the corner of his mouth with his napkin then turned his attention to Lise. "I could say it's my brilliant deductive reasoning, but I will admit it's because I saw you coming out of the hotel." He shrugged. "And because people who are from here know I own this place."

Now that wasn't expected. A man with his looks and build seemed suited to endeavors much more exciting than scooping ice cream. But then, he did have his nephew Andrew to perform that task.

Her left shoe slipped, and she reached down to shove it back on her foot. As she straightened, she found the Dip Cone's owner studying her intently.

"Now that you know what I do, what do you do?"

Lise took another taste of the sweet treat then dabbed at her mouth with a napkin. It wouldn't do to have ice cream running down her chin while in the presence of the possible middleman. "I'm an architect," she said when she'd accomplished the task.

His smile slipped a notch. "Is that so? Would you happen to work at Restoration Associates in Houston?"

She nodded. "So you've heard of us?"

"You could say your reputation precedes you." Abruptly, the man rose. "Now if you'll excuse me, I've got somewhere else to be right now."

Lise scrambled to follow, trying in vain to look audacious and keep her sandals from slipping off. "Wait," she managed when she'd dumped the remains of the cone in the bright red trash can situated outside the front door.

The man halted and turned to face her. Somewhere between the table and the door, he, too, had tossed the ice cream. Now he stood with his hands stuffed into his jeans pockets in a stance that looked more linebacker than Dip Cone owner.

"What is it, eh?" he said in a voice thick with the local drawl. Funny, it hadn't been there before.

She stood for a moment, wavering between turning to walk away and righting whatever wrong she'd inadvertently committed. "What did I say?" she finally managed.

"It's not what you said." Uncle Ted paused and let out a long breath before resuming his walk. "It's who you are," he called over his shoulder.

Fast as that, the middleman was getting away. Not only that, but somehow her reputation had garnered a black mark. What reputation, she had no idea. Nor did she know what she'd done. Lise shuffled toward him then gave up and kicked off her sandals in order to catch up. "I don't understand."

"No, I suppose you don't, although I think you'll have a clearer picture tomorrow."

"Tomorrow?"

"At the presentation." He stopped in front of what looked like an old bank building then loped up the stairs two at a time to stab a key into the door. Above his head on the transom window was a clue to the puzzle.

There, in old-fashioned gold letters below the logo declaring this building the headquarters of BTG Holdings, were the words TED BREAUX IV, ARCHITECT.

five

Tuesday, on the way to City Hall

Ted walked the three blocks to city hall with his necktie and his conscience chafing. His behavior last night was atrocious, and he had no excuse. Sure, the woman worked for the company that sought to raze most of downtown Latagnier and turn it into a shopping mall, but that gave him no reason to act the fool.

Always be the better man. That's what his father had told him from the time Ted could tag along behind him.

And last night he'd failed at that.

Once this business of awarding the contract was over, he'd make good on an apology. Maybe he'd even take her to lunch at a place that offered more than ice cream. Surely a big bowl of shrimp gumbo and a slice of pecan pie would ease the sting of losing the contract to him.

Ted picked up his pace, warming to the idea. He passed the darkened windows of the Dip Cone and managed a smile. The thought of owning the place where so many of his childhood memories were made never failed to cause a reaction.

"Mornin', Ted," the town vet called as he wheeled by on his bike. Several other townsfolk greeted him by name, as well, including dear Miss Bessie McCree, the owner of the now-closed Latagnier Preschool, who'd taught the alphabet and good manners to him and most of the citizens in Latagnier now over the age of thirty.

"Nice hat, Miss Bessie," he said as she scurried by, no doubt heading to her volunteer post as Latagnier's sole crossing guard at the elementary school.

"Your aunt Peach told me today's the big day," she called over her shoulder. "I been tugging on the Lord's ear for you this morning. I can feel it in my bones that something big's going to happen."

Something big. Whichever way the Lord allowed the day to go, the result would definitely be something big.

"Thank you, ma'am," he said as he shifted his briefcase to the other hand. The thought of his gently refined aunt Peach broadened the smile. As soon as the dust settled on his morning, he'd have to pay her a visit. That would be a treat. On a good day, lunch with Aunt Peach was almost like having his mother back—at least for an hour or two. On a bad day, she still provided him with a link to Latagnier that he'd almost let go.

On any day, she was worth listening to for the entertainment value alone. When Peach got going on a subject, it was a certainty that she'd be chewing at it awhile, often with great passion.

He ducked into the courthouse and slowed his pace, switching gears to put his attention on the task at hand. Despite hearing from city hall insiders that Restoration Associates had all but bought the mayor's loyalty, Ted refused to believe he would not be awarded the job. After all, his roots ran deep here.

Taking a deep breath, Ted shoved open the door and stepped inside the combination auditorium and courtroom. A fair number of city folks sat in the audience, including several former mayors—all, it seemed, associated in one way or another with the Breaux family.

Ted greeted them all, offering handshakes to uncles and male cousins and quick hugs to the female family members. Finally, he reached the auditorium stage.

"Come on up here, son," Mayor Harlon Dorsey called from his spot at the head of a long conference table sitting center stage. "Soon as all parties are in attendance, we'll get started."

The mayor, short in stature and thick through the middle, had outdone himself today. This being his last official duty, he'd not only donned his fanciest church clothes but also sported a red carnation in his lapel.

It all added up to a great effort on Harlon's part, but then, he always did like to go overboard. As much as the mayor would like to be remembered as a legislator of some importance, Ted had never managed to forget that for many years Harlon Dorsey served as the town's dogcatcher.

Likely his popularity with the townsfolk had not been affected by his change of occupation. But then, when no one opposed you, victory was always assured.

"Nice flower, Mayor," Ted said.

The older fellow grinned and leaned toward Ted then grasped his hand in a firm handshake. "From my wife. Seems as though she thought to celebrate the importance of the occasion. Of course, if no one steps up to run for my seat, I just may have to disappoint her and stay in office another term."

The formalities over, Ted took a step back and winked. "Well, let's hope that doesn't happen."

He gave Ted a sideways look. "What does that mean? Don't you think I've made a good mayor for the city of Latagnier?"

Well aware that the contract of a lifetime swung in the balance, Ted held his tongue and forced the truth into submission. "What say we ask your constituents?" Ted turned to the audience. "Let's hear it for our mayor as he leaves office."

A smattering of claps and a few choice comments were the only responses. Ted leaned closer. "See, they're overwhelmed at the ending of an era."

Ignoring the comment, Harlon gestured to a pair of empty chairs at the end of the table. "Sit yourself down over there and wait until you're called on, Breaux."

He complied, choosing the nearest chair. Once he'd settled his briefcase down beside him and placed the rolled blueprints in front of him, Ted glanced up at the clock that had kept time over civic meetings since the Depression.

Five after nine. As his gaze swung away from the clock, he watched Bob and Landon slip in the side door. Bob grinned as Landon gave Ted a thumbs-up. Before Ted could respond, the door swung open with a crash and in tumbled his competition.

Looking a bit too flushed to have walked slowly, the Restoration Associates representative paused to adjust the shoulder strap on her oversized briefcase then stepped inside, a roll of what were surely blueprints under her arm. Ted smiled in spite of himself. Never had drab navy business attire and a take-me-seriously hairstyle looked so good.

The woman must have taken his smile as a greeting, for she returned it then pressed forward. Mayor Dorsey bounded off the stage like a man half his age and met the lady architect halfway.

A second later, the mayor trotted back with the prints in hand. Somehow he managed to set the bundle down and pull out the woman's chair in one swift move. Ted could only watch and pray the amusement he felt didn't show on his face.

Then he saw it. Harlon Dorsey winked. And it wasn't at him.

Right there in front of half the city of Latagnier, the mayor had the gall to wink at a woman who was not his wife.

Ted sat up a little straighter and watched as Mayor Dorsey bustled away toward the microphone. After taking a swipe at his upper lip, the mayor tapped the mic with his forefinger then wrapped his hand around the base.

Failing to adjust the height to his stature, Harlon finally lifted the mic off the stand and pointed it toward the city secretary, who, unfortunately, sat just to the left of the speakers. The resulting shriek came from both the amps and the secretary, who bolted from her chair and upset the table of handouts she'd been collating.

Bolting toward the mess, Ted righted the table then began shoveling papers into a stack. Soon the pile had been transferred to the tabletop where the city secretary began the task of reassembling the minutes from last month's meeting.

"Good work, Breaux," the mayor said as Ted stepped past him.

A nod was all Ted could manage with a sarcastic comment teasing his tongue. He settled back into his chair and straightened his tie. The last thing he wanted was to look like a fool in the newspaper tomorrow.

❧

Lise held her breath as the mayor opened the meeting with a prepared statement regarding the state of the city and his intention to stay on as their mayor unless someone came forth to claim the title. During the latter minutes of the speech, which according to the clock went on for more than a quarter hour, Lise stopped watching the politician and started watching her opponent.

Covertly, of course.

The man who had displayed such courtly manners in the ice cream parlor—at least until he discovered that she was the competition—certainly did not look the part of a small-town fellow. Rather, his expensive suit and polished demeanor marked him as someone who had spent a great deal of time outside this tiny burg. The briefcase sitting next to his fancy boots likely cost ten times more than hers, and the designer logo looked out of place in the simple surroundings.

Uncle Ted caught her looking, so she darted her attention back toward the podium. As the mayor waxed poetic on the benefits of living in such a splendid city, Lise went over the major points of her presentation in her head. First she would compliment the townsfolk on a past rich with history, and then, in an ordered progression of bullet points, she would usher them into the future—their future. At every conceivable opportunity, she would stress the small amount going out of the city's coffers in payment for the miracle she would perform and the large returns that miracle would bring.

All right, so maybe *miracle* wasn't the best word choice. Still, Lise hoped to do amazing work in downtown Latagnier. So amazing that even the grumpy local architect would give her praise, even if it came grudgingly.

She also planned to show Ryan exactly how foolish he had been to leave such a talented and intelligent woman. Lise smiled at the thought.

In his last meeting with the firm, Mayor Dorsey had warned Ryan that any opposition to the change that must take place would come from the citizens who'd lived in Latagnier the longest. Chief among them, he predicted, were certain members of the large Breaux clan.

Lise frowned. Surely Ted Breaux was not one of those backward folks who opposed anyone with forward-thinking ideas.

"And so, without any further delay, I present the two contenders for our downtown renovation project. Please hold your applause until I've announced both candidates."

"Oh, come on, Harlon," an elderly woman called from the shadows of the back row. "We know who Ted is, and we know who this gal isn't. Just save us all some time, eh, and announce Ted as the winner of this horse race, won't you?"

Mayor Dorsey shielded his eyes and leaned to peer in the direction of the voice. "That you, Peach? You got somethin' to say you think's more important than what I'm sayin'?"

"You know very well it's me, Harlon." A thin woman dressed in a rose-colored tracksuit stepped forward. "Hey there, Teddy, hon," she said as her spiky gray tresses caught the light. "We been praying for you, sweetie."

Out of the corner of her eye, Lise saw Ted's shoulders slump.

"That's enough now, Peach. I can't just hand this contract to Ted. I've got to make this fair and square. You hear?"

Peach rested her hands on her hips and gave him what amounted to a schoolteacher look. That much Lise had learned in her brief time as an education major.

"Oh, come on, now," the older woman said. "You been doin' what you've pleased ever since the good folks of this town gave you the job of mayor. What do you mean you can't just give my Teddy the job?"

Ted slid a sideways glance in Lise's direction and mouthed a curt, "Sorry."

She responded with a what-can-you-do? shrug.

After all, she knew too well what it felt like to be on the receiving end of a woman bent on seeing to your best interest. The only difference between Mother and this Peach woman would have been in what they wore to the assembly. While Peach looked svelte and put together in her casual outfit, Mother wouldn't have been seen in such auspicious surroundings without pantyhose and proper high heels—white before Labor Day and anything else after.

Someone in the audience began to clap, and soon it became painfully obvious which of the two the crowd preferred. Lise tried not to take offense, and yet the applause for her opponent stung.

This time the small-town architect didn't bother to apologize. Rather, he seemed to be enjoying the accolades.

"Attention, people," the mayor called. "I'm gonna need your attention right here and right now. You've all had a chance to see what these two have planned for our city. At least those who cared enough to read the proposals that were turned in last month."

"Yeah, I read 'em," an older man in the front row said. "That gal there wants to turn our downtown into a shopping mall like they've got over in Baton Rouge. I don't know about the rest of these folks, but there's a reason I live in Latagnier instead of Baton Rouge."

"And I'd like to keep it that way." Ted rose and pointed to the man. "Thank you for bringing that up, Doc Villare. I'm sure the other proposal is a good one—for someplace other than Latagnier. I, for one, think any change to the historic district would be detrimental to progress."

Lise could stand it no more. "I disagree," she said as she stood. "Restoration Associates approaches all our projects with a certain sensitivity to the local population."

"Is that so?" Ted crossed both arms over his chest and stared down at Lise. "Explain how turning our buildings into a glorified outlet mall is exhibiting a certain sensitivity to the local population. And then there's the plan to tear down the hardware store." He turned to the crowd. "Is there anyone in this room who doesn't remember what it was like to walk the aisles of that place? Are we content to let that slip away like so much else that's gone?"

"You tell her, Teddy," Peach said. "And don't forget to mention how we all feel about turning the old funeral home into that fancy underdrawer store."

Underdrawer? Lise stifled a smile as she realized Peach referred to the upscale chain store that had been in discussion to acquire retail space for its exclusive lingerie line. On several occasions, Lise had tried to get Ryan to understand that that possible tenant was one that did not represent the shopping demographic.

"That client has not been confirmed." She bristled. "And to

clarify, there's not to be an outlet mall. What we're doing is offering a combination of retail and residential in a walking-shopping configuration. If you'll look at the proposal, you'll see—"

"What I see is a lot of mumbo jumbo about things I don't understand," another man called. "There's just one thing I do understand. Ted Breaux is one of us. I'm sure you're a nice woman, ma'am," he said, "but we don't know you."

"No, but I've studied—"

"People, please," the mayor shouted.

"I have a plan," Ted said above the noise, "that will allow Latagnier to use its downtown space without losing it. As sure as I'm standing here today, I pledge to fight any plan that will alter a single brick on those downtown buildings."

"Forget this, Ted," someone called. "Run for mayor and then you'll have control of the whole shebang."

"Now that might not be a bad idea," he said. "What do you think, Mayor Dorsey? Maybe I should just take your job, and then I'd be able to do what I want with downtown."

"It doesn't work like that, Ted," the mayor said. "I have final say, yes, but there's still the matter of—"

"Mayor Breaux!" someone called.

"Mayor Breaux!" another responded.

Soon half the citizens were chanting and the other half looked as though they wanted to. Meanwhile, Harlon Dorsey looked as if he might throttle someone at any moment.

Lise seemed to be the only person in the room without an opinion.

"Now that's quite enough," Mayor Dorsey finally called. In lieu of a gavel, the mayor banged the microphone on the podium. The resulting clunking noise did a much better job of silencing the crowd than the verbal attempts of the mayor.

Lise returned to her seat, and Ted followed suit. While she watched the mayor, her opponent seemed more interested in what was going on in the audience.

Even Peach decided retreat was a good idea. Lise watched the woman settle back into her seat. With a shake of her head, she leaned to the left and said something to the woman beside her. Whatever transpired, the pair seemed in agreement as they both nodded.

"All right, now," the mayor finally said. "I thought we might have a civil meetin' here today. Seein' as some of you"—he paused to lean over the podium and stare in the direction of the boisterous Peach—"don't care for the rules of order in this town, I am forced to—"

"Now that's not true, Harlon." Peach rose. "You know good and well I waited to be called on."

Mayor Dorsey shook his head. "I never called on you."

"Oh yes, you did." Peach looked to those around her for support and found it in abundance. "You called me by name and asked me flat out if I had something to say that was more important than what you were saying." She touched her chin before offering a dazzling smile. "And, well, I did."

Laughter and applause blended until the mayor raised the microphone again. "Sit down, Peach," the mayor called.

"You did ask," Peach said in her defense.

"I did at that." The politician offered the crowd his best vote-for-me smile. "And as you know, I'm always open to hear the opinions of my constituents." A long pause, and then he continued. "Just not today. I declare, by the power vested in me by the citizens of Latagnier, Louisiana, that the contract for gussying up our downtown goes to Restoration Associates, most ably represented by the lovely Miss Lisa Gentry." He banged the microphone once more. "Meeting adjourned."

The man she'd formerly thought of as a potential middleman now sat in what appeared to be stunned silence. Eyes that yesterday seemed the color of warm chocolate slowly turned in her direction. The look on his face made her glad she now stood in a crowd of witnesses. Unfortunately, these seemed the sort of folks who might forget what they saw should the hometown hero be accused of anything untoward.

For a moment, Uncle Ted seemed to have lost his voice. "Congratulations, Lisa," he finally said as he thrust his hand in her direction.

"It's Lise," she squeaked out, "not Lisa."

"Does it matter?" he snapped. A moment later, his expression softened. "I'm sorry. I shouldn't have said that."

Lise was about to respond when the mayor came over and captured her attention and her hand. "Come with me," he said. "We've got contracts to sign."

"Yes, well, I wonder if I shouldn't tell the folks a little more about what our team's planning to do with their town. I mean, if they just understood, then maybe—"

"Let's just get this over with," the mayor said. "Like as not, this isn't the time to convince anyone of anything."

She gave up trying to speak and meekly followed the mayor out of the chaos and into the relative quiet of his private office. As the door shut behind them, Lise thought she heard the voice of Ted Breaux speaking to the crowd.

six

Two months had passed since Lise first set foot in Latagnier, Louisiana. With the infamous Fortieth Anniversary Party behind them, the constant topic of conversation with Susan nowadays was the ongoing discussion of potential middlemen.

Lise didn't dare tell her sister she'd thought for a moment that the architect back in Latagnier might be the fabled middleman. If she so much as mentioned a name, she would never hear the end of it.

It was just as well she didn't, given the result of that town hall meeting back in September. With the crisp fall wind blowing from the north and the miles falling behind her, Lise knew that thinking of anything but the renovation project would be a lapse in judgment of monumental proportions. Thus, her search for the middleman would have to wait until after downtown Latagnier had been spiffed up and polished to a shine. Gone also was her search for her audacious side.

For now, she was back to the old Lise. The Lise who cared more for comfort than accessorizing. Working in the office these past eight weeks had been difficult, to say the least. With the only man she'd loved—emphasis on past tense—in an office next to hers, she spent her days avoiding rather than seeking out the man who signed her salary checks. In their unavoidable weekly staff meetings, Lise chose the chair closest to the door and farthest from Ryan, often excusing herself at the end of her presentation on the pretense of pressing business.

Truthfully, the Latagnier project had kept her busy, so the need to keep her time away from her desk as short as possible was grounded in necessity as well as emotion, especially in the past few weeks.

Lise sighed. For the last week, it seemed as though there had been one snag after another. From tiny annoyances like subs who didn't answer their phones to major issues like permits that were refused and inspections that resulted in failures, the list grew each day. Thus, rather than wait until January to schedule her arrival in Latagnier, Lise decided to make the move early in order to supervise the work herself.

She remembered marching on shaky legs into Ryan's office to make the announcement. Since their breakup, she'd only entered his office once, and that had been to deliver a letter on a day when he was out of the office. The difficulty of saying the well-rehearsed lines was eclipsed only by the disappointment she felt when she looked into Ryan's eyes and saw only relief.

Armed with the thought that Ryan was actually happy she would be out of the office, she amended her intention to leave after Thanksgiving and told him she'd be gone as of Monday.

A greater temptation had been to tell him she'd be gone permanently. Thankfully, she'd resisted that urge.

Up ahead, the exit sign for Latagnier loomed. From the highway, a left turn took her to the two-lane road that led right through the middle of town. In less than ten minutes, she passed the first landmarks that signaled she'd reached her destination.

This time, Lise drove past the oddly furnished Bayou Place Hotel rather than into its parking lot. As the job would require a lengthy stay, Lise elected to take up residence in the nearest available dwelling to the job site in downtown Latagnier. She reached across the seat for the paper upon which she'd written the address.

The little home on Post Office Street, aptly named for

its proximity to the town's postal facility, would serve as her office as well as a place to hang her hard hat during the long days ahead. If the problems that had arisen were any indicator, there would be many of those long days.

Already a few snags had appeared in her seamless plan. Several permits that had been guaranteed by the mayor were being pulled and reexamined. In addition, the inspections were not going as planned. In fact, as of yesterday, there had been no inspections of the first of several properties on the schedule.

Then there was the issue with the hardware store. Evidently a vocal minority had laid claim to the promise that they would keep the building from being demolished. Mayor Dorsey seemed oblivious to their concerns. At least, neither she nor Ryan had heard anything from him despite multiple e-mails and a few unanswered phone calls.

Were she not completely sure that the Lord had her exactly where He wanted her, Lise might have panicked. Rather, she'd packed her things and headed to Latagnier, bound and determined to overcome whatever obstacles lay ahead.

Even as the leaves had begun to fall, the moss-bedecked evergreens still wove a beautiful tapestry across the horizon. Their presence signaled the edge of the bayou. This much she'd learned from the chamber of commerce's Web site.

What she did not yet know was what that bayou looked like, although she hoped to find out eventually. Too bad Latagnier Realty hadn't been able to locate a rental near it.

She imagined a flowing stream, much like the lovely tributaries she'd witnessed during summers at camp in Colorado. Or perhaps it was more like the frigid waters of the Frio River near the central Texas towns where she'd often sought solace in the dark days after Ryan's defection.

Given her schedule, it might be weeks before she would know the answer. And still, it seemed completely criminal to come to southern Louisiana and not see the bayou for herself.

Up ahead, the single-story redbrick building with the American and Louisiana flags flying in the stiff breeze signaled the location of the Latagnier post office. Situated just to the left was a lovely whitewashed Victorian cottage on a small slice of green city acreage. Three trees decorated the shell driveway, and a lush bed of pansies and spiky monkey grass greeted her.

Lise pulled her SUV into the drive, the shells crunching under tires that would not see the Houston freeway again until the obligatory Christmas trek home. Already Mother had begun complaining about her impending absence from the traditional Thanksgiving feast and subsequent viewing of the A&M versus University of Texas football game. Even the reasonable explanation that she could not walk away from a job site less than two weeks into the job would not suffice.

"But that's another story for another day," she muttered as she threw the gearshift into park and shut off the engine.

Odd. Where had she heard that statement before?

Somehow it stuck in her mind, although the provenance remained fuzzy all through the unpacking process. Finally, she tossed the worry away along with the question and determined to forget all about it. After all, tomorrow was the first day of the rest of her career.

Lise sighed. "How lame am I to take perfectly good sentiments and turn them into something that applies to the only thing I have going in my life: work?"

Fishing the key chain from Latagnier Realty out of her bag, Lise pressed the button on the garage door opener and waited for it to rise. Giving up on the third try, she stepped out of the car and walked to the porch to let herself into the cottage.

Someone had come recently to air out the structure, as

evidenced by the scent of pine cleaner and the note written on Latagnier Realty stationery and tacked to the ancient Kelvinator. While the fridge hummed with the effort of keeping its interior cool, the furnace kicked on in an attempt to warm the rest of the place.

She set her purse and keys on the counter and went to retrieve her things. While Restoration Associates had leased the place for six months, Lise hoped to be back in Houston much sooner than that. The most recent schedule had the completion date set for late February, but Lise, a veteran of projects such as this one, knew to add at least six weeks to any projected goal.

Thus, she would be home before the bluebonnets bloomed. But for now, she needed to concentrate on the present. To that end, she reached for the note and dialed the number for Latagnier Realty. Failing to reach anyone, she left a message regarding the garage door opener then walked back outside to retrieve her bags.

By the time Lise finished hauling her things into the tiny bedroom at the top of the stairs, she had little need for the heater. Still, she knew better than to turn the thing off, given the potential for disaster that came with ancient appliances. Rather, she chose to slip into her favorite worn, torn, and well-loved maroon sweatpants and Texas Aggies sweatshirt. Padding downstairs in her slippers, she decided to brew a cup of tea and take it to the back porch, where a view of the stars surely awaited.

Resting her head on the back of the old wooden rocker, Lise fought the urge to close her eyes and give in to the rest her body craved. Instead, her eyes remained open, bypassing the silver crescent of the moon to scan the skies for the constellations she and Troy often counted as children.

"Orion, the Big Dipper," she said as she dug her toes deeper into the comfortable slippers with the Collie-shaped head of the Texas A&M mascot emblazoned on each one.

A falling star zipped across the sky and disappeared behind a stand of pines in the distance, taking her breath with it. "Dreams come true when you wait on the Lord," she whispered. Words her father spoke over every falling star they'd witnessed together.

If only she were ten again.

Lise shrugged deeper into her sweatshirt and hugged her knees to her chest. The empty mug clattered to the floor and rolled in a crooked path toward the edge of the uneven porch. Rather than chase it, Lise watched the mug disappear over the edge and land in the soft grass. She would pick it up later; right now any move might shatter her pensive mood.

Slowly, she placed her feet on the porch boards and set the rocker in motion. Allowing her eyes to drift shut, Lise let out a long breath and listened as the symphony of the night began to rise in song around her. Crickets, frogs, and the occasional night bird played the melody, while a barking dog provided a staccato harmony.

In a matter of minutes, or perhaps it was hours, the rush of city life that had thrummed through her veins since her return to Houston in September fell away, and a new, slower rhythm took its place.

"Heavenly," she whispered and then rested from the effort.

"Mais oui. C'est tres bonne."

The deep voice sent Lise pitching forward. Something tangled with her arm, and she tugged at it. In the ensuing struggle, Lise landed facedown with something heavy sitting atop her.

"Fire!" Lise called in the show-no-fear-even-if-you're-terrified voice she'd learned to master in self-defense class. "Fire!" she repeated for good measure.

A moment later, the attacker relented, and the weight on her back disappeared. Lise scrambled to her feet, losing one of her slippers as she clawed at the screen door. Finally, it swung open, and she fell inside.

"You all right?" someone called.

"Get a description," she said between gasps, "then call 911. I'm locking myself in."

A long shadow darkened her door as a heavy footstep made the old boards creak. She slammed the lock twice before it caught on the ancient door frame. Even then, its reliability was uncertain at best.

Lise began to pray.

"We don't have 911 in Latagnier, but I'd be glad to get the fire department if you think that rocker's going to burst into flames. Otherwise, I'd say you're safe for tonight."

Doubled over from the effort, Lise pressed on the screen door and fumbled for the lock. From her vantage point, she spied a pair of dark boots. Her self-defense training kicked in once again.

Faded jeans with a hole in the left knee. Long legs. Leather jacket, dark brown. Hands in pockets. Possibly holding a. . .

"Fire!" she called again. "Fire! Fire! Fire!"

The perpetrator took a step forward then stopped just short of the doormat. A hand rested on the outside of the door then pressed against the screen. "Settle down, there, Lisa. I was just trying to be neighborly."

Something in the voice caused a memory to bubble to the surface. Her heart still hammering in her chest, Lise allowed her gaze to drift upward until it landed on the shadowed face of someone who looked awfully familiar.

Cheekbones that could have been cut from granite supported a grin that turned to laughter while she watched. A cleft in his chin and a dimple only on the left side of his smile could only mean one thing.

"You're not—I mean, you didn't because you're. . ." Still gasping for air, Lise lifted her gaze a notch higher to meet the amused stare of her attacker. "Uncle Ted?"

The architect chuckled again. "I supposed I'd answer to that in some circles, but most folks just call me plain old Ted."

She straightened and held one hand to her heaving chest while supporting herself against the door frame with the other. "What in the world were you doing skulking around here? You scared me to death."

He shrugged, his face a mask of boyish innocence beneath dark brows. "Me? Nah, it's that rocking chair you've got to watch out for. From the tussle I witnessed, you're lucky to be alive. You gave it a good go, though, especially when the flames broke out."

Lise looked past him to where the chair in which she'd been relaxing a moment ago now lay on its side. Heat began to climb from her neck into her cheeks as the realization dawned on her.

"The rocking chair? You mean there wasn't a. . ." She paused to collect her thoughts. What an idiot she'd been. "So why exactly are you here?"

"I brought you this." Ted reached into his pocket and withdrew an envelope. "Should I leave it under the mat, or are you willing to open the screen enough for me to slip it inside?"

Her hand trembled as she fumbled with the latch. "What is it?" she asked as the contents of the envelope shifted in her hand.

"The new garage door opener."

The return address stated the envelope came from Latagnier Realty, and someone had written TENANT AT 210 POST OFFICE STREET across the center in big letters. "But why did you bring it?" she asked to his retreating back.

The architect answered with a wave of his hand as he took the back porch steps two at a time and disappeared into the darkness that was the backyard. Lise fished in the drawer for a pair of scissors then cut off the end of the envelope. Sure enough, a small black garage door opener fell into her hand.

Lise leaned against the door frame and weighed the remote in her palm. A press of the button and she could hear the garage door groaning into motion. A second press and it stopped.

"How about that?"

"I told you so, Lisa."

She jumped, and the remote clattered to the floor. Ted Breaux once again smiled from the other side of the screen.

"Stop sneaking up on me," Lise said as she scooped up the remote.

"I thought you might want this, Cinderella." He thrust her slipper toward the screen then shook his head when she only opened the door enough to slip her hand out and grab it. "Life's too short to be so suspicious, city girl."

Ignoring his comment, she chose a polite, "Thank you," instead. Setting the shoe on the floor, Lise slipped her foot into it. "And for the record, I'm not suspicious. I'm just safe."

Straightening, Lise half expected to find he'd gone again. Instead, he was busying himself righting the rocker and setting it back in place near the rail. While she watched, he fell onto his knees and leaned over the edge to retrieve the mug she'd lost earlier.

Without comment, he set it on the mat and turned to leave.

"Thank you," she said again.

This time he stopped, although he did not turn in her direction. A gruff, "You're welcome," was all he said before disappearing into the night.

A thought occurred, and she opened the screen to lean halfway out the door. "Hey," she called into the chilly air.

"What?" came the response from the shadows.

"Since when are you the guy who drops off garage door

openers? I thought you were an architect."

His response was a hearty laugh and the sound of boot heels on the sidewalk. "So did I," drifted toward her as the sound of his footsteps turned the corner onto Post Office Street and faded into the night.

seven

Lise settled behind her borrowed desk in the construction trailer and eyed the stack of papers and memos littering its surface. Though it was well past eight and the sun now streamed through the high, east-facing window, the space still held a chill. She inched the zipper up on her sweater and curled her fingers into the pockets for a moment of warmth before setting to work.

Several pages caught her attention, and Lise moved them to the top of the growing stack. Chief among them were three that bore the stamp of the city inspector along with a big red check in the box labeled FAILED.

She pulled the specs and printed off the file then clipped them to the letter from the inspector. A couple of the items the man flagged were legitimate issues, but the rest were frivolous at best. Lise's sigh released a puff of frosted breath into the brisk air.

Her first instinct was to call the inspector and nail him on the items she intended to dispute. Likely that would only make matters worse, especially if the fellow was one of those old-school types who disliked working with women.

Indeed, given the locale and the distance from any reasonably large urban area, the odds were good that she'd encounter that kind of opposition.

"So how to proceed?" She toyed with the knotted cord of the ancient black telephone then jumped when her cell phone rang.

A check of the display showed a familiar number. Ryan. She put on her most official tone. "Restoration Associates. This is Lise."

"Hello, Lise. How's your first day on-site going? Are they treating you well?"

She sucked in a deep breath then let it out slowly before testing his name on her lips. "Ryan. How nice of you to call and check on me."

She cast a sweeping glance around the claustrophobic, unheated trailer then pasted on a smile despite the fact that Ryan was on the phone and not standing before her. Somewhere along the way, she'd read something that said your facial expression was often reflected in your voice. Well, if so, then Ryan Jennings needed to hear how very happy she was. Even if that wasn't exactly how she felt.

"Things are going fine." To emphasize her casual tone, she leaned back then grimaced when the chair springs squealed in protest. "Nothing I can't handle," she quickly added as she righted the chair.

"Glad to hear it." He paused. "I must admit I've had my reservations over allowing you to do this alone."

"You have?" His admission stunned her then, a second later, made her mad. "Are you saying you don't think I'm capable? I would certainly be surprised to hear that coming from you."

"Oh no, no. That's not it at all. It's just that, well, Latagnier isn't Houston, you know?"

Exactly. She held the phone a little tighter.

"And it's not like I can rush over and help if I'm needed."

Oh, how very much she wanted to tell him exactly how little she needed him. The thought, novel as it was, surprised her with its truth.

Despite the statement, Ryan proceeded to begin his usual discussion on what he would have done had he been the one on-site. Lise set her phone down atop the outgoing mail pile and pressed the SPEAKER button.

At once, Ryan's deep voice filled the trailer. "Who's there with you, and why can I suddenly hear them?"

"I have you on speaker so I can take notes." Lise reached for pen and paper then thought better of it. "And the voices you hear are outside the trailer. Subcontractors amusing themselves."

The chatter had ebbed and flowed outside the door for more than half an hour, at times loud and other times only a murmur. Voices raised in conversation seemed to alternate between English and some variant of French. Sometimes the words sounded like neither.

At present, she heard nothing but laughter. On any other site, she would have turned them all off the property, but as Ryan said, this was not Houston.

Ryan. Lise returned her focus to her mentor and listened politely as he offered advice on dealing with those he referred to as "country folk."

"So as long as you don't stand out too much, you should be fine. Just spend the first couple of days on-site watching and listening. Listen to the old-timers. They know the best subcontractors." Ryan paused. "But you know that."

"Yes," she said. "Just go along. Listen to my elders. Take notes. You taught me well."

Silence fell between them, and for once Lise did not rush to fill it. Let Ryan wonder if there was some double meaning to her statement. She already knew there was.

"The office has been quiet without you," Ryan finally said.

Now that was unexpected. Lise drummed her fingers on the desk then reached into the desk drawer for a pen. A lime green sticky note attached to the front of the drawer caught her eye, and she lifted it off.

" 'Texas, don't mess with Latagnier,' " she read aloud.

"Excuse me?"

"Oh, I'm sorry, Ryan." Lise replaced the note on the drawer and leaned forward to rest her elbow on the stack of inspection forms. If someone wanted to discourage her from working on the project, this note was a juvenile and ineffectual start.

"What does that mean? 'Texas, don't mess with Latagnier.' Are you speaking in code now?"

"Code? No." Lise checked her watch. "But I do need to cut this call short. I'm sorry. I've got an appointment with the mayor in ten minutes, and I need to go over some of these specs before I try to argue my case regarding the inspections."

"So the mayor can overrule a city inspector?" Ryan asked.

"That's my understanding."

"Interesting. But then, I guess that's the way small-town politics works."

"I'm not sure this is politics." She reached for the specs. "But I suppose I'll know more once I speak to Mayor Dorsey."

"Oh, didn't you know?"

"Know what?" The door opened, and in walked the last person she expected to see on a Restoration Associates job site: Ted Breaux.

Hard hat in hand, the local architect pointed to the empty chair across from her, and she nodded. While he settled himself, Lise switched the phone off speaker and returned her attention to Ryan.

"Dorsey's not the mayor anymore," Ryan continued. "We barely slid our project in at the end of his term. It was quite the coup getting the plans approved so quickly and without changes."

How well she remembered. Still, nothing had been said regarding a replacement, so she'd assumed he'd stayed on as he'd mentioned he might do.

"We're still okay, though, right?" she asked then cringed. It would not do for Ted Breaux to assume that there was some sort of weakness in the Restoration Associates ranks.

Ted Breaux checked his watch then reached for his cell phone, his expression less than pleasant. Of all the nerve. Lise was tempted to prolong her phone call until the local architect gave up and left. Unfortunately, that would require talking for an extended amount of time with Ryan.

She chose the lesser of the two evils. "Ryan, I've got someone here. I'm going to have to get back to you on this."

"Sure, sure," he said. "But please understand I'm here if you need anything." He paused. "And I do mean *anything*."

Now it was her turn to ponder double meanings, although she decided to postpone it until later when she could give the subject her full attention. For now, she had another pressing agenda: getting Ted Breaux out of her office before the mayor arrived.

The last thing she felt like dealing with this morning was another debate between Ted Breaux and whomever had taken over for Mayor Dorsey. She also preferred that the man sitting before her did not see the stack of paperwork from the inspector.

The less Ted Breaux knew about her troubles, the better.

She closed the phone then set it aside. "Sorry." Lise gestured to the phone. "Headquarters calling. So. What can I do for you? In the five minutes I have left before my next appointment, that is." She paused as realization dawned. "Oh, I get it. You've come to explain your mysterious visit last night. Maybe even apologize for causing all that trouble?"

He stiffened. "Apologize? Me? Look, I was just there to do you a favor."

"About that. What were you doing with my garage door opener?" She gave him a hard look. "I know it's a small town and everyone's related to everyone else, but surely the town architect doesn't make house calls for missing garage door openers that don't belong to him. And if you do, well, frankly, I find that just plain creepy."

His dark brows went up. "Creepy? I guess I can see how it might appear that way. What you should probably know is that I don't deliver garage door openers for just anyone. I do happen to spend quite a good portion of my time carrying out my duties. Oh, and I happen to be a pretty decent architect with more work than I can handle, as well."

She relaxed a notch. If this guy was a stalker or some sort of social misfit, he certainly did a good job of covering for himself. "You still haven't told me how you came to have my garage door opener."

"Oh, that." He shrugged. "My father owns the place, but he's on the road. I generally handle things at the shop while he's gone."

"The shop? As in Latagnier Realty?" Lise stifled a groan. "So you're my landlord?"

Ted seemed to think a moment. "I suppose I am, at least until Pop returns." His grin broadened; then he had the audacity to wink. "I hope you're not one of those tenants who has me over unclogging sinks in the middle of the night. People might talk."

It was all Lise could do not to roll her eyes at the ridiculous man. How had she ever thought *he* of all people might actually be the middleman?

He glanced over his shoulder at the half-open door then leaned forward. "I know I'm early, but if you wouldn't mind, I'd like to go ahead and get started."

"What are you talking about?" Lise shook her head. "I have an appointment with the mayor. My office set it up last week."

"Yes," he said slowly, "I know."

"You know?" She rose, and Ted Breaux followed suit. "Honestly, Mr. Breaux. I know this is a small town, but, well, I'm trying to do my job here. I know you thought you could do it better, but the mayor chose me. Now if you'll excuse me, I'm going to wait for the mayor out at the job site."

"Hold on a minute," he said. "Sit back down. I think we need to get a couple of things straight."

In her experience of dealing with difficult contractors, Lise had learned to wait them out—to give the indication that she would listen while they spoke. From the look on this man's face, it was time to go into that mode.

"Fine," she said as she slowly lowered herself onto the chair. "Go right ahead and straighten me out, but keep in mind I've got a meeting in"—Lise made a show of leaning to look past him at the clock—"three minutes." She crossed her arms over her chest and leaned back. "Go ahead, Mr. Breaux. You've got the floor."

The Breaux fellow's expression relaxed slightly as he sat down. "First off, I don't just *think* I can do a better job of this renovation; I know it. You're a stranger here. This is my city, my home." His voice rose as he warmed to the topic, and he looked as if he might jump from the chair and begin pacing at any minute. "Where you see architecture, I see buildings where my grandmother used to trade eggs for groceries and my great-grandfather used to buy nails to build the old schoolhouse. This place has a history, and you don't have a clue what that history is. All you want to do is make this project something you can stick in your portfolio."

Lise held her temper—barely. Much of what he said about her was true, but what was wrong with a great portfolio?

When he relaxed his stance and went silent, she seized her opportunity to leave the confines of the small room. Once again, she pointedly glanced at the clock. "Well, Mr. Breaux, I'm sorry, but my time's up. I've got someone important coming, and I need to prepare."

"Important?" Another grin, this one sending a dose of merriment to his chocolate-colored eyes. "Really?"

"Yes, really."

He shifted positions. "How important?"

"Extremely. In fact, it would be rude to keep someone in his position waiting, so if you'll excuse me. . ."

She reached for the pile of memos and began to scan them,

more as an act of dismissal than out of any real need to read them. When she'd shuffled through the same pile again, she noted with irritation that the man still sat across from her. Finally, she'd had enough.

"Mr. Breaux?"

The dark brow lifted once more. "Yes?"

"If you don't leave, I'm going to have you removed. I've been polite and listened, but I fail to see what further business you have here, so would you please leave?"

"Can't do that. I have a meeting." Dark eyes met her stare. "With you." He swiveled to look at the clock then checked the time against his watch. "In exactly thirty seconds."

"Wait." A thought began to take flight, and along with it came a cold dread. "Oh, please don't tell me—"

"That I'm the new mayor of Latagnier?" He nodded, and the dimple returned. "Sure am, Lisa. As of two weeks ago. Oh, and don't forget—I'm extremely important, so it would be rude to keep me waiting."

❧

Ted couldn't help watching the lady architect's flustered expression with anything but satisfaction. Indeed, the tables had been turned. Restoration Associates might have the contract, but in Latagnier, the mayor had the final say on almost every aspect of the project.

A lesser man might call the whole thing to a halt and insist on a new round of bids. Unfortunately, the Lord and Ted's accountability buddies had already set him straight on that prospect.

So here he sat, watching Lisa whatever-her-name-was squirm.

And for the life of him, he could take no further pleasure in it. Sure, it was great to have the upper hand. If only he didn't have to answer to his conscience.

The object of his thoughts met his gaze with eyes the

color of the Latagnier sky.

"Lise," she said.

He shook his head. "Excuse me?"

She pushed away from the desk and rose. "My name is Lise. L-i-s-e. Lise Gentry."

"I see." The gusto with which she corrected him made Ted smile. "Then I owe you an apology, *Lise*."

"Apology accepted."

Ted watched his host reach over and yank a hard hat off a row of pegs then jam it on her head. The effect was not altogether unpleasant, although it took Ted a moment to get over the transformation. From their first meeting at the Dip Cone, when she wore an unforgettable yellow dress, to the day she squared off against him in a no-nonsense business suit and old-lady shoes, the Texas architect had proven her ability to shine in whatever outfit she put on.

His mind drifted to last night. She'd made a sweatshirt and a pair of faded maroon sweats accessorized with dog-head slippers look like a million bucks. But today, well. . .

Ted gave her a covert glance, hoping his appreciation for what jeans and a trim denim shirt did for her was not written all over his face. Evidently his secret was safe, for Lise snagged her keys and made for the door without so much as a backward glance. "Coming, Mayor?"

"Where are we going?"

"I assume you'll be wanting a tour," she said just before the door slammed behind her.

Palming his own keys, Ted yanked the door open and stepped into the sunlight. "Right behind you," he said, "but you're going to have to ride with me, or the tour's over before it begins."

She whirled around so fast he almost ran into her. Peering up at him, she seemed on the verge of either a giggle or a groan. "You're not serious."

Standing his ground, Ted set his jaw and returned the stare. "Serious as a heart attack."

"So you're one of those men who feels his masculinity is in question unless he's in complete control of a motor vehicle." She offered a smile that didn't quite make the journey to her eyes. "Let me guess." Lise pointed in the direction of the spot where Ted had parked. "That big black monster with the gun rack and running boards is your truck."

"You're saying it like there's something wrong with that." Ted followed the line of her sight and picked out a particularly feminine-looking sedan. A hybrid, no less. "Well, I'm certainly not going to ride in something like that. It's yours, right?"

"Actually," she said slowly, "mine is the red one parked next to your Bubba-mobile."

Bubba-mobile? Before he could take offense, he caught sight of her vehicle—a brand-new, four-wheel-drive SUV with all the bells and whistles, exactly like the one he'd had his eye on since reading about its debut in *Car and Driver* last year.

At the time, he'd even considered trading his truck in for one. In red.

"Sweet," he said under his breath, even as he gave thanks he hadn't had the bad sense to purchase the same vehicle as someone so obviously opposite of him. "I hear that baby rides like a Caddy and tears up the dirt like a John Deere tractor."

For a brief moment, Ted could have sworn he saw a smile cross her lips. Then, as quickly as it appeared, it was gone.

"Yeah. Look, I could talk cars all day, but I'm supposed to be showing you around and getting you up to speed on what we're trying to accomplish here." Lise cocked her head to the side and crossed her arms. "Tell me. How can I do that if you're driving?"

A valid question, and yet Ted had long ago given up riding in a car with a woman at the wheel. In fact, the last woman he'd ridden with had been the school bus driver, a woman whose license surely had been purchased by mail without benefit of instructions or a driving test. The day he got his first truck, he'd walked off that bus after school and vowed never to subject himself to that sort of torture again.

Many years had gone by since then, and his record remained perfectly intact. He'd not ruin it for the likes of her.

"It's my city, I'm driving, and that's final." He clicked the alarm on his truck and turned his back on the bristly woman. "Coming?" He fired the words in her direction without giving her the satisfaction of halting his pace or turning to look at her.

Either she fell into line or she walked away. Either option was fine.

Besides, if she walked away, then the coast was clear for another firm to take over the job.

eight

Lise overcame the temptation to return to the trailer and let the pompous mayor go solo, but only because she knew it would be a worse-than-rocky beginning to what was bound to be a long relationship.

Working relationship, she quickly amended. He, after all, was *not* the middleman.

The mayor had the motor purring before she managed to heft herself up inside. Her practiced gaze took in the interior with reluctant approval. As four-wheel-drives went, this one was a classic. Were it not so much fun to tease him about the truck, Lise might have asked him a thing or two about how it handled and what sort of mudding he'd done with it.

Instead, she did as Ryan instructed and kept quiet, allowing the mayor to interrupt the silence with the occasional sparse comment about the locale. In the span of three minutes, they'd waited through the city's only traffic light then come to a stop in front of a coffee shop aptly titled the Java Hut.

In one of the blocks that combined the gentrified charm of crumbling Victorians and sparkling storefronts, the Java Hut stood out as the sole business open at this hour. The door opened, and a man walked out carrying a tray with four covered cups.

Ted threw the gearshift into park and waved to the man. "He's a good one to know," Ted said. "Best plumber in Latagnier. Nobody knows the quirks of the city's sewer system like T-Boy."

Again she nodded rather than comment. T-Boy? What kind of name was that? Not that it mattered. Her subs were all in place, and it was unlikely she'd need more. Still, she bit her tongue rather than tell the mayor this.

"All right," he said as he killed the engine. "Your tour starts here. Let's go."

"Wait," Lise said. "We don't have time to waste on coffee. I've got a busy day ahead of me. And I'm sure you do, too," she amended.

He looked at her as if she'd said something blasphemous. "Stick with your tour guide," he said as he opened the door. "I'll see we get everything done that needs doing."

She climbed out of his truck in front of the Java Hut and scrambled to keep up with the new mayor's long strides. "Still, I fail to see how a cup of coffee is going to accomplish anything," Lise said as she stepped up onto the curb and hustled to follow her host.

The infuriating man finally slowed his pace enough to allow Lise to catch up then reached ahead to open the door for her. "See," he said slowly, "that's your problem. You've only got one point of view. I'm here to open your eyes to another way of looking at things."

Wonderful. Lise shook her head as she stepped into a coffee-scented haven that looked as if it had begun life as a feed store. "I appreciate that and all, but—"

"Hold that thought." Then he was gone—off to mingle with a crowd that obviously considered him a minor celebrity.

Running the gamut of backslapping, handshaking, and smiling citizens, the mayor finally arrived at the counter where a pair of smiling young women greeted him. Lise found a table in full view of the festivities and made herself comfortable.

A few minutes later, he broke from the crowd carrying two steaming mugs. One of the baristas trailed in his wake carrying a tray containing two empty plates and a pile of sugar-doused pastries. She set it in the center of the table with a smile.

"Anything else?" she asked the mayor.

"Thanks, but this ought to do it."

"All right, then." Never sparing Lise a glance, she turned on her heels and sashayed back to the counter, her ponytail swaying.

"Pay attention, Lise. The first lesson of living in Latagnier is to learn how to appreciate café au lait and beignets." Ted slid one of the mugs toward her then offered a plate from the tray. "Take one of those." He pointed to the pastries. "That's a beignet."

She did as he told her then rose. "She forgot the forks. I'll go get—"

"No, she didn't forget." He pointed to the chair. "Sit down and hear me out. Eating beignets is not for the uninitiated. If you do it wrong, you'll miss the best part. And you sure can't appreciate the finer points of this delicacy without getting powdered sugar on your fingers."

The door jingled, and someone called Ted's name. He looked over and waved then returned his attention to the pastry. "This is how you do it. First you pick it up. Try not to breathe in while you're holding it."

Not breathe? How odd.

With his free hand, Ted positioned the coffee mug beneath the pastry then took a bite. Flecks of powdered sugar landed like snow atop the caramel-colored coffee. When he was done, his smile and the tablecloth were dotted with sugar. He slapped his hands together then swiped them on the napkin in his lap before reaching for another beignet.

"For me, it takes two of these before I'm ready for the coffee. You might not care for it to taste so sweet, but I like it that way myself." Brown eyes twinkled with what looked to be merriment. "It's all personal preference. Now you try it."

Lise attempted to take a bite out of the delicacy but sneezed when the sugar flew upward instead of sprinkling the coffee as Ted's had. She set the pastry on the plate and reached for her napkin.

"What did I do wrong?" she asked from behind the protection of the white cloth.

"You inhaled." He shook his head and illustrated with another bite and another delicate blizzard of powdered sugar atop the coffee. "I warned you about that."

"You did?"

"Yes, I did. The best way to eat beignets is by holding your breath until you've taken a bite." He gestured to the remainder of the pastry. "Now get back up on that horse and ride it again."

She gave him a questioning look.

"Sorry," Ted said. "That was a favorite expression of my last coach. What I mean is, grab another one and give it a taste. You won't be disappointed."

Lise tried again and this time somehow managed to get the powdery donut inside her mouth before incurring any further embarrassment. Ted smiled as if he'd just witnessed something as momentous as her first baby steps.

"Well?" he said before she'd stopped chewing.

"Well," she responded as she reached for her mug. "It's definitely sweet."

He looked as if he expected further comment. She took a sip of the coffee concoction. True to his warning, the coffee had been sweetened by the powdered sugar, but something else had been added to it.

"Milk?" she asked as she took another sip.

Ted nodded. "Hence the name, Lise. Café au lait. Coffee with milk."

"All right," she said. "I remember a little from my high school French classes."

Her companion grabbed his third pastry from the dwindling pile and downed it with gusto. "I don't suppose you've figured out that the French you learned isn't the same language we Cajuns speak, have you?"

"Actually, I did wonder why I only recognized about half of what the subs were joking about outside my door this morning."

He cringed. "That's probably for the best. Like as not, the jokes weren't meant for a lady to overhear. I probably ought to speak to whoever was loitering and carrying on. Did you happen to hear any names?"

Once again, he caught her off guard. Evidently chivalry was not dead in this remote corner of Louisiana.

"That's not necessary," she said. "I can take care of myself."

He leaned back in his chair and dabbed at the corners of his mouth. "I'm sure you can," he said as he leveled an even stare in her direction, "but nonetheless, if there are men who need reminding how to act when a lady is present, then I am offering to do that."

A lady. Lise almost laughed. She'd been referred to by numerous names during her decade in the construction field, but this was the first time someone had called her a lady.

She almost told him so, but another of the many citizens of Latagnier had captured his attention and was bending his ear about some civic matter of great importance. While Ted was occupied, Lise enjoyed another beignet.

"And this is Lise Gentry," Ted said, swiveling to gesture toward Lise. "Lise, this is Howard Collier from the *Latagnier News*."

Lise set her mug down and shook the newsman's hand. They exchanged pleasantries for a moment before the men went back to their conversation.

The bell over the door jingled, and a pair of well-dressed women walked in. When they spied Ted, the pair stopped in their tracks.

A bit of arguing seemed to go on between the women

before the blond shook her head and the brunette frowned. Finally, they stopped talking and started walking—toward them.

Funny, but they weren't looking at Ted when they stopped just out of his line of sight. Rather, the pair had their sights set on Lise.

⋙

Just about the time the newshound let him off the hook for an interview, Ted saw the dynamic duo. What the *Latagnier News* didn't know about the goings-on of the city, these two did. Neither could be called a gossip by any stretch of the imagination, but both shop owners seemed to attract customers in the know.

Likely the word was already out that he'd been seen with a strange woman this morning at the Java Hut. The only question was which one called the other.

"Neecie, Bliss. What are you ladies doing out and about so early this morning?"

Without waiting for an invitation, the pair helped themselves to the two remaining chairs at the table and made themselves comfortable. "It's not early," Neecie Gallier said. "I've already cooked five breakfasts, made five lunches, and sent four kids off to school. You know Landon. He's always the first one on the job site, so he was off before I ever got the kids out of bed."

"That's right," Bliss Tratelli said. "And I've been up since the crack of dawn baking six dozen cupcakes for this afternoon's teacher appreciation tea at the elementary school. Thank goodness I talked Bobby into staying home this morning and watching the babies. You know how they love helping me with the frosting."

Neecie nodded. "And after all that, I still had an early fitting."

"Really?" Ted managed.

"You'd be surprised how many brides want to come in before work and try on their dresses." She paused to stifle a yawn. "You know I'm not a morning person, but how can you say no to a woman in love?"

Bliss tapped Neecie on the shoulder and giggled. "Honey, you know as well as I do that Ted doesn't know the answer to that question." She turned to Ted. "Do you, Ted?"

The conversation shift took Ted by surprise. He was still working his way through all the things these women had already accomplished this morning. He was tired just thinking of it.

"Ted?" This from Neecie.

"I, uh, well—"

"So." Bliss turned to Lise and smiled. "I'm Bliss Tratelli. My shop's the Cake Bake a few blocks down."

"Lise Gentry." The lady architect grinned. "I know that place. The exterior is exquisite. Did you do the restoration?"

"No, she didn't," Ted said. "BTG Holdings spruced it up this summer. Perhaps you've heard of the company?"

"It is great, isn't it?" Neecie leaned toward Lise. "I'm Neecie Gallier, and I own the bridal shop next door to the Cake Bake."

"Yes," Lise said. "In the old pharmacy building, right?"

"Exactly," Neecie said. "You've done your homework."

Lise met Ted's astonished gaze. "I try."

Before he knew what happened, the women had all introduced themselves, lamented over Ted's perpetual state of singleness, and sent the object of their discussion to the counter for more beignets and fresh mugs of café au lait.

It was enough to make him tired—and terrified. Fetching coffee and beignets seemed the next safest option to making a run for the door. It also gave him some time to think of a good way to get the lady architect back into the truck and the tour back under way.

What had he been thinking, making a stop at the most populated morning gathering place in Latagnier?

Ted ended up in line behind Howard but kept his attention away from the newsman and on the budding conversation back at the table. For some reason, it felt more than a little dangerous to have those three make an acquaintance. When Lise smiled, he really began to worry. Surely the Lord wouldn't allow a friendship to grow between such an unlikely trio.

"Looks like the lady architect's made some new friends."

He turned to nod at the newsman. "Yep," he said. "It surely does."

"Are you worried, Ted?" Howard asked.

"Worried? Me?" He shrugged. "What do I have to worry about?"

"Well," Howard said slowly, "as a reporter, I'd have to start with the facts. You know there's never been an unmarried mayor in the history of the city. And those two, well, you also know they've made a project of trying to fix you up since the day you came back to town." He grinned. "I'd say those two items add up to a plan that ought to make front-page news if it succeeds."

"Don't be ridiculous, Howard," Ted said as he shrugged off the possibility with a roll of his shoulders. "Lise Gentry is here to fix up downtown. The only reason I'm keeping an eye on her is to see that she doesn't mess up the city I love."

Howard's thick brows shot up. "If you say so, Ted." He nodded toward the table where Neecie and Bliss were handing the lady architect their business cards. While he watched, Lise reciprocated.

"Oh, this can't be good," Ted muttered. "Not good at all."

The newsman only chuckled.

nine

Ted returned to the table with more beignets and two steaming mugs and two cups of café au lait to go. Carefully setting the tray in the center of the table, he reached for one of the paper-wrapped cups and made to hand it to Lise. "You might want to add sugar to this since we'll not be taking beignets in the truck."

Lise started to stand and reach for the cup, but Bliss's laughter stopped her.

"You know, Ted, if you were as particular about other things as you are about that truck, well. . ." Bliss gave an exaggerated sigh. "What am I talking about? He *is* that particular. Lise, you should have seen his place in Baton Rouge. You could eat off the floors, I swear."

"Hey now," Ted said, raising his hands in a feeble protest. "Unlike some of you at this table, I don't have any ankle biters running around leaving oatmeal on the furniture."

"Ankle biters?" Lise shrugged. "What's that?"

"Don't pay any attention to him," Neecie said. "That's his pet word for children. It's what he calls anyone under the age of fifteen. See, he has this germ phobia and—"

"Wait a minute. I do not," Ted said. "I love kids, and you know it."

Neecie nodded. "We're just giving him a hard time. He really does have a way with kids. You should see him with Bobby and Bliss's little ones. The twins follow him around like he's the Pied Piper."

"Still," Bliss said, "Ted, you must admit you're a clean freak."

"I am not." He looked to Lise. "Ignore them."

"Oh, really?" came Neecie's quick response. "What about the time that you, Bobby, and Landon were out duck hunting and. . ."

Lise watched the exchange with interest. Two minutes into the conversation, she'd figured out these women were the wives of the mayor's business partners at BTG Holdings. What she hadn't yet figured out was what they were doing cozying up to her. Surely they knew she was the one who now worked the job the new mayor had bid on.

Instinct said they'd decided to keep their enemy close by, but something else—their refreshingly open and friendly personalities, perhaps—told her she was wrong. It seemed, on the surface, as if these women were genuinely trying to befriend her.

The mayor tapped her on the shoulder. "Sugar?"

"What?" Lise jumped at the overly familiar endearment. A second later, she realized he held two packets in his hand. "Oh." Embarrassment flamed her cheeks, and she looked away. "No, thank you. I think I'll pass."

Somehow she managed to make her exit without allowing her discomfort to show. Ted Breaux opened the truck door and held her coffee while she climbed in then handed it to her. "Ready for the grand tour?"

The "grand tour," as it turned out, was a drive down six blocks of downtown Latagnier with a running commentary on which relative or family friend built which building. It seemed as though he was carefully saving the block where her first project was under way for last. The block that included the one building she'd listed as needing total destruction and rebuilding. As much as he'd indicated his displeasure at making changes to his beloved city, tearing down the old hardware store likely did not sit well with the new mayor.

To Lise's surprise, however, he turned left at the intersection just before the parking lot where her SUV sat, leaving the construction project and downtown Latagnier behind. She slid him a sideways look. "Where are we going?"

"To where it all began," he said as he signaled to turn left onto what turned out to be a winding country road.

Had the man not held the office of mayor, she might have been a little concerned by the fact that he now seemed to be driving right into the middle of nowhere. Surely someone as well liked as Ted Breaux would not do something crazy.

Lise reached for her cell phone and checked for service. Four bars. She breathed a sigh of relief. Still, maybe she should call the office and let them know where she was.

"Worried?"

She glanced up to see the mayor of Latagnier alternating between studying her and watching the road. "What? Um, just seeing if the phone works."

He laughed. "Go ahead and make your call if you'd like. We've got another few minutes until we get to where we're going."

Caught, she had no choice but to dial her secretary in Houston. By the time she'd been updated by the chatty woman, the truck had come to a stop.

"Thanks, Kim," Lise said as she hung up.

"All caught up?" Ted asked.

The oddest feeling of guilt swept over her as she nodded.

"Good, then let's go." He shut off the engine and bounded out the door to race around and help her step onto the soft ground.

"You didn't have to do that," she said, secretly glad that he had all the same.

"Stay close," he said as he turned toward a stand of trees. "There's a path, but it's a narrow one."

"That's what the Bible says," she quipped.

The mayor paused but did not face her. "Yes," he said slowly as he resumed walking, "it does."

Something in his tone sounded uncharacteristically gentle. Odd, coming from such an exasperating man.

Still, this was the wilderness.

Lise halted. "I'm not so sure," she called.

This time he turned around, and his face wore a careful rather than impatient expression.

"You're perfectly safe with me, if that's what you're worried about."

As she followed his broad back down the path, Lise could see little of what lay ahead. To her left and right, sparse, thin grasses gave way to a thicket that looked nearly impossible to cross. Despite the November chill, the sun felt warm on her back.

Rolling her shoulders, she eased the tightness left over from a night of tossing and turning in an unfamiliar bed. Up ahead, Ted stopped abruptly then stepped to the side. Beyond where he stood was a clearing. Lise craned her neck to see what held the mayor's attention. As she came upon the scene, she smiled.

There, in all its slow-moving glory, was Bayou Nouvelle. At least she assumed it was.

"It's more beautiful than I expected," she said as she brushed past her host before tearing her attention away from the chocolate-colored water. "Is this the Nouvelle?"

He nodded then gestured to a spot a few yards away. There, a bench had been placed in the center of a crescent-shaped clearing. "Come and sit with me." He met her stare. "And, yes, this is important. I'll have you back in a half hour, forty-five minutes at the latest, but right now I'm ready for our meeting." He paused. "Welcome to my other office, Miss Gentry."

Lise eyed the bench then glanced down at the time on her phone. "All right. As long as we can keep to that timetable, I think I'm okay."

She made the statement as if she actually had plans for the afternoon. In truth, the day was wide open, marked only by this meeting and the time to leave and go home. Until the plans were signed off on by the mayor and the inspections reapproved by the city inspector, she had very little to do.

But Ted Breaux did not need to know that.

"This is lovely," she said as she settled onto the bench. In truth, the setting was divine, all lush greenness and amber leaves that fell like random snowflakes onto the water's murky surface.

"It is that," he said softly. "I'm glad Bob thought to put this bench here. It's a good spot for sitting."

Lise remained silent, preferring to listen to the swish of the leaves in the fresh wind and the call of some persistent bird in the distance. Above her, the sun climbed, but the temperature did not. She inhaled the earthy scent of clean air and felt peace settle into her bones.

If Ted Breaux were not sitting beside her, she'd surely fall into a sound sleep right here. Perhaps another day she would find her way back to this lovely spot. She made a note to watch the turns and road signs on the way back so she could do just that.

"So, lady architect, are you ready to hear the story of Latagnier?" He leaned forward, elbows on his knees, and stared out at the water. "You've seen the buildings, but it's not complete until you know the people who built them. The ordinary, God-fearing folk who made their livings and lived their lives behind the brick and mortar you're about to mess with."

The statement begged no answer, so she kept quiet. Likely half the town, maybe more, thought as he did. A convincing argument for change could not be made until she'd heard the argument against it.

Ted Breaux did not disappoint.

"That water there is not just a river on a map." His deep voice blended with the rush of brisk wind to warm and chill at the same time. "It's why the town is here. A hundred years ago, the Nouvelle was used just as much as that road we drove down. It was as likely you'd float into Latagnier by pirogue as arrive by horse or buggy." The mayor swiveled to look at her. "Do you know what a pirogue looks like?"

She shook her head.

"It's long and flat and shaped a little like a teardrop. The Acadians, they did with what they had, so most times their pirogues were constructed from cypress logs. Nowadays they're generally made of fiberglass. There's an old Cajun saying that a pirogue can float on heavy dew." He chuckled and returned his attention to the flowing water. "That's not far from the truth. A well-made pirogue can get around where most other boats can't. They're adaptable, you see, and made to fit the place where they're used."

"Interesting." She watched his shoulders heave and wondered if perhaps she'd missed the point in this brief history lesson. What did boats have to do with buildings?

"It's more than interesting, Lise."

"Okay."

He rose but made no move to step away from the bench. "Adaptability: That's a part of our culture. We've learned how to make things work here, how to take what we have and make it fit what we need." He looked down at her, his expression shadowed. "And that has everything to do with what's going on downtown."

"I see." Lise rose as much to lessen the gap between their heights as to hurry their exit. "So given the history of this town, how can I make what I'm doing fit what you believe the town needs? And keep in mind, we *do* have approved plans."

"Yes, you do." The truth of how little he appreciated the

reminder was obvious. "But I am still the—"

"Yes, I know. You're *still* the mayor." Lise bit her lip as regret hit. "I'm sorry. That was rude."

He let the statement and her apology pass without comment.

"You want to know what you can do?" He reached out to snap off a twig and studied it. "Stop trying to make this city what it isn't." The mayor let the twig drop then turned his attention to Lise. "Latagnier's not a big city, never was. All these fancy plans and expensive stores, well. . ." He looked away. "That's like putting lipstick on a pig. When you're done, it's still a pig, but likely you've made a mess in the process."

Lise took a moment to try to process the analogy. Failing that, she pressed on with her case.

"My plans are to make it better, not different. I've said that from the beginning, and the blueprints back it up. Most of the work we're doing is on buildings that would have fallen down sooner rather than later." She pressed past him and moved toward the path. "So if you don't have anything else to show me down here, I suggest we get back to town. The morning's almost gone, and I've got a desk full of paperwork waiting for me."

He snagged her elbow then released it a second later. "There's one more thing I'd like you to see." Reaching into his pocket, he withdrew his keys. "But you're right. I have taken up far too much of your time. On top of that, my bum knee's acting up. Must be the change of weather. We'll make that trip another day."

"All right," she said, although she found herself oddly curious as to what else the now-limping mayor might want to show her.

Probably some other structure his family either built or lived in. If Ted Breaux was to be believed, his family was responsible for anything put together with hammer and nails.

Lise followed the Cajun back up the path, her conscience jabbing her with each step. She'd been rude, but worse than that, she'd broken her own rule: Listen before speaking. As she slid onto the seat and buckled the restraint, Lise tried to think of a way to make amends.

"So," she said after a mile of bumpy road was behind them, "one of the items on the agenda today was to discuss the visitor center. I wonder if you might like to talk about it now."

"About that."

He slowed to ease the truck over a nasty hole in the road then pulled over in the grass and threw the gearshift into park. Lise's heart sank. Was there nothing about this project that the mayor of Latagnier liked?

"Yes?" she said in what she hoped was an interested but not concerned tone. "What about it?"

The mayor swiveled to face her, his expression impossible to read. "You realize that was Latagnier Hardware for many years."

A statement, not a question. Still, she nodded in response.

"And you further realize that what you're proposing will completely remove any signs of what that structure used to be. A whole lot of happy memories gone in a pile of dust all to make way for something I'm not convinced this city needs."

"That's not exactly how I would put it, Mr. Breaux, but I can see how you might think that way."

"It's the truth, Miss Gentry, and there's no sugarcoating the truth."

"I disagree. Wait. What I meant is, I do not agree that the city doesn't need a visitor center." She paused to collect her thoughts, a difficult proposition considering the man she once thought could be the middleman stared at her as if she were a child in need of educating.

"I can see we're not going to agree on this. I believe by sandblasting the exterior and removing the rotten wood, we're not only preserving the bones of this structure, but we're also repurposing the building for the better use of Latagnier's citizens." He paused to grip the wheel. "And that is what you are paid to do: repurpose and preserve."

His response hit a nerve. "That's the purpose of the entire renovation. However, you must admit there are some structures that, while still sound, are too expensive within the parameters of the budget to keep intact."

"You are being paid to preserve." Proof of his rising temper showed in his white-knuckled grip on the steering wheel. "Tearing down the hardware store does not preserve, and I won't allow it."

"Mr. Mayor, surely you would not. . ." Lise paused to gather her wits once more. What was it about this man that sent her pulse pounding? "Surely your loyalty lies with your constituents."

"It does." His determined look sharpened. "However, I fail to see how gutting the building is going to please the voters of Latagnier. You can repurpose and preserve without removing any sign of what the building used to be."

Lise frowned. "The problem is, the building's interiors are unsalvageable."

"I disagree." He shook his head to accentuate the statement. "I know the upstairs apartment was modernized in the 1970s because a buddy of mine from back in junior high lived there for a time, but other than a couple of layers of linoleum downstairs, nothing much has changed."

Was he kidding?

"That structure has been subdivided and altered so much over the past hundred years that there is little left to the interior. It was a disgrace what the former owners allowed to happen. Did you have any idea what the place was used for?"

she asked, warming to the topic. "As far as I can tell, it looked and smelled like it had been taken over by cats and used for their comfort, if you know what I mean."

"Really?" He leaned against the seat. "I had no idea. I know there was a pet store on the first floor for a while, but that place closed probably five years ago."

"Evidently someone forgot to tell the pets. I swear they were still living upstairs in that 1970s apartment you remember. It was awful." She shook her head. "Didn't you notice the smell when you did your walk-through?"

The mayor looked away. "I thought I knew what was inside the structure, so I didn't. . ." He seemed to gather his thoughts. "The structure's a good one. What's inside is fixable," he said, although his words seemed as much a question as a statement.

An awkward silence fell between them. It became painfully obvious that Ted Breaux had missed an important detail in the creation of his plan.

Lise knew she could have used the moment to her advantage, first by pointing out the obvious deficit in his knowledge then by challenging his commitment to flexibility in the planning process. Instead, she let the chance slip by and changed the subject. "You haven't mentioned the building we're turning into a bookstore. I'm sure by now you've seen the updated plans."

He turned back to face the steering wheel then shifted into drive. "I have."

Uh-oh. Not the most enthusiastic tone.

Dare she ask? *Oh, why not?* It wasn't as though she'd made any sort of favorable impression on him so far. "And?"

Signaling to turn, he waited until they were up to speed on the highway before responding. "Did you find any signs of rot in the facade? Termites? Water damage?"

Lise thought a moment. "No, I don't recall any. In fact, the structure was one of the better preserved ones on the list."

"And yet you're asking me to approve pulling off the entire facade?" He slowed to allow a faster-moving car to pass. "I fail to see how you can justify removing perfectly good late-nineteenth-century gingerbread trim. I've seen the plans. An awning is not an acceptably correct replacement for an authentic overhang like the one you're intent on destroying."

This she could handle. The answer was clear, the solution brilliant. So brilliant, in fact, that she'd been saving the news for the next time she wanted to prove her skills to the mayor.

From the look on his face, now was the time.

"Do you know what that millwork fetches on the open market? By selling off the exterior trim work and replacing it with the canopy the bookstore's owner is asking for, we not only please the tenant, but we also make back enough to offset some of the city's costs. Thus, it's a matter of civic responsibility."

As soon as the words were out, Lise longed to reel them back in, such was the scowl on the mayor's face.

The protest she expected, given his expression, never came, nor did the negative comments or snide remarks she figured would accompany it. Rather, Ted Breaux drove down the highway as if he were on any other midmorning commute to the office. For a good five minutes he spared neither a comment nor a glance in her direction. The only sign of discord came in the white knuckles he'd created by gripping the wheel with such intensity.

Lise should have enjoyed the reprieve. She should have, but she did not. Her brilliant plan to use the millwork to pay for a good part of the reconstruction had failed to be appreciated by the one person whom it helped the most. Coming in below budget gave more back to the city's coffers, thus making Ted Breaux look like a million bucks.

Well, a few thousand anyway.

Still they drove, slipping past lush meadows and thickets of cedars and pines with the only sound coming from the heater that blew a steady stream of warm air across her chilled legs. Lise shifted from shadow to sun and let the light bathe her face. Another few minutes and she might have fallen asleep.

For a Bubba-mobile, the truck was mighty comfortable. And for a grouchy politician, Ted Breaux drove quite safely. She slid a glance in his direction and noticed he'd donned a pair of dark sunglasses, the kind men wore at the beach or out snowboarding.

The better to hide your eyes, Ted Breaux, she thought.

Only the discontent over being misunderstood and denied her moment of brilliance stirred Lise to action. First, she attempted to catch his attention by clearing her throat and shifting positions. Failing that, she decided to try direct confrontation.

"I take it you disagree," she finally said.

No response. This time his silence continued all the way into the parking lot where he pulled his truck in next to her SUV. Lise gave in to the male pouting, and by the time she reached for her purse, she almost found it amusing.

Almost, but not quite.

He shifted into reverse and held his foot on the brake. So he wasn't staying. Obviously, the mayor did not intend to continue their meeting back in her office.

Lise pressed the button to release her seat belt then gripped the door handle in one hand, her purse in the other. "Care to hear my apology or my explanation first?"

"Neither," he said.

She opened her mouth to comment, but he held up his hand. Choosing to comply, Lise clamped her lips tight and gave him her attention. Perhaps he was actually going to apologize to her.

Maybe even acknowledge her brilliant plan to sell off the millwork. In a perfect world, he might even thank her.

He seemed to study the floor for a moment then turned in her direction. "We're both professionals here. If you think you need to send pieces of our town history off for sale on the open market, who am I to disagree?"

Again she opened her mouth to answer. Again he silenced her with a look.

He snapped his fingers as if he'd forgotten something. "Oh, wait," he said. "That's right. I'm the mayor. I *do* have the right to disagree. Not only that, but I can open an investigation into your financial practices that will shut down your work in a heartbeat. Maybe you'd like to have my office go through your books *and* your blueprints. What do you think of that, Miss Gentry?"

"I think we've come a long way since double dark chocolate caramel ice cream with red hots, Mr. Breaux." Anger flushed her cheeks. "And to think I actually thought you were nice."

He laughed, but there was no humor in it. "And to think I actually thought you were a decent architect."

ten

As soon as he made the statement, Ted knew he'd gone too far. What was it about this woman that caused him to speak first and regret it later?

From their first meeting at the Dip Cone, she'd been nothing but an irritation. How they would manage to work together on this or any other project was beyond understanding.

Ted was about to tell her just that when the lady architect pointed her finger at him.

"Think what you will about my abilities as an architect, but I can see things with a much clearer perspective than you can right now, and the reason is one you've pointed out more than once: I'm not from Latagnier."

"That's the truth," he muttered, still unsure of allowing himself to say more.

Lise heaved a sigh and seemed to be as upset as he was. Taking this field trip had been a bad idea. A really bad idea.

He might have been better served having Bea send over a brochure from the Latagnier Chamber of Commerce. At least then he might not have to admit to Bob and Landon the behavior he'd exhibited in the last hour.

If only he'd realized all of this before he locked himself in the truck with this madwoman.

Ted reached over and unlocked the door. To that end, he also shifted the vehicle into PARK. The last thing he needed to do was to make a statement by storming out of his truck only to watch it crash into the construction trailer.

Yeah, that would be a statement, all right.

He was about to shut off the engine when the Gentry

woman shook her head. "Look, here's the bottom line: Your town is dying, Ted Breaux."

Dying? As bad as the words stung, Ted knew there was truth in them. Wasn't that why he'd returned? To try to save what seemed to be slipping away?

To revive what was dying?

"And if you're going to take on the job of mayor with any level of seriousness," she continued, "you're going to have to accept the fact that there will be compromises. Without them, you run the risk of bankrupting the town you profess to love so much."

Bankrupt Latagnier? How dare she accuse him of such a thing! He had run for office to save the city he held so dear.

Or had he?

"Look," he said slowly as he fought to keep from losing the struggle to control his temper, "I think we ought to talk about this after I've had some time to consider things. Why don't you work on an alternative to selling off the trim work, and I'll work on reserving my judgment until I've read your new proposal and seen the revised blueprints."

"New proposal?" The words came out as a thin squeak.

He couldn't tell if she was angry or upset, but she certainly didn't hold him in as high regard as she had when their day together began. No, he amended, she was both angry and upset. She likely thought better of the dead bug squashed on the front license plate of her fancy SUV.

Looking at his passenger again, he began to feel a little like that bug. Minding his own business one minute and smashed flat the next. Hit without warning for no reason and yet wondering what he could have done to prevent it.

Ted let out a long breath. "Look, you don't have to start from scratch. Your basic design is good. Just go back to your original premise and tweak it."

"Tweak it?" Now the color rode high in her cheeks. "Are you serious?"

"I am." He released his death grip on the steering wheel and flexed his fingers to return the blood to the tips. "It shouldn't be difficult for an architect of your caliber to come up with a plan to keep the millwork on the old bank and hold down the budget at the same time."

"Anything else you'd like me to add while I'm *tweaking*?"

She said the word with more than a little derision in her voice. Ted's first urge was to comment on her attitude and remind her of his superior position as mayor. Given his track record with controversial statements, however, he knew better than to broach the subject.

Besides, she obviously had no illusions about the sort of mayor she believed him to be. Better to just get on with the discussion and leave his credentials—and his ability to squash her project like that license plate bug—out of it.

"No," he said in what he hoped would be an even tone. "Not that I can think of."

"And the hardware store?" she ground out. "Would you like a new proposal on that structure, as well? Perhaps one that does no damage to your precious 1970s apartment? After all, we can't have what's best for the city intruding on your happy memories."

Well, that does it. "Yes, please do. And I just decided that the budget's going to be slashed by half, so take that into consideration. I'm going to need the money for the deficit on the bookstore project."

"The deficit?" She said the words slowly, seemingly attaching meaning to the statement only after repeating them. In an instant, her expression changed from stunned to serious. "I wonder, Mr. Mayor, if you would like to set the appointment time for our meeting now."

"The appointment time?"

She had him there. He'd expected an argument, not such easy compliance. Surely she was up to something. But what?

Ted recovered in an instant and returned to his all-business attitude. "Yes, well, I'll have my secretary call you."

"You have my number?"

Leaning forward, Ted stared at the woman over the top of his sunglasses. "Oh yeah, Miss Gentry. I definitely have your number."

She leaned against the door, obviously missing the double meaning in his response. "Fine."

He pressed his sunglasses back into place. "Fine."

Ted watched her open the door and climb out. Stupid as it was, he frowned when he realized he hadn't gone around to help her. As the Gentry woman stalked toward the trailer that served as her office, Ted decided that his choice to remain as far from her as possible until they both calmed down was likely a good one.

And as for holding a meeting with her, well, he'd have to think on that. Likely he'd not find a way to get out of the apology he'd surely owe her, although for the life of him he couldn't figure out exactly where he'd gone wrong in the conversation.

What had begun earlier with the simple intention of instructing the lady architect on the history of Latagnier had quickly become a battle of wits. There was no accounting for the female temperament. Then again, he knew too well that the bad behavior of others did not excuse his own.

Ted leaned back against the seat and closed his eyes. "Lord, what is it about spending time with that woman that turns me into someone I don't even like?"

He contemplated the question for a full minute, maybe two, then decided the answer would not be quickly forthcoming. Generally, he heard the Lord best out on the bayou in his grandfather's pirogue, but today his schedule did not allow him that option.

For that matter, there wasn't a day this week or next that

he could just be alone with God. Ted opened his eyes and sighed as he threw the gearshift into reverse and backed out of the parking space. Somehow the idea of coming home to save the city—and himself—just wasn't working out the way he'd planned.

Another sigh and he found himself on the road headed toward his office. It wasn't far—a five-minute walk in a stiff headwind—and he drove it as slow as he could without holding up traffic.

Not that there was much traffic in downtown Latagnier these days. "Something I plan to fix unless dealing with this Texas tornado gets the best of me first."

Bypassing his secretary, who thankfully was fielding phone calls, Ted closed the door to his office and stood against the worn wood with his hand still on the old brass knob.

"I'm going to have to talk to the guys about working on this lack-of-time thing, aren't I, God?" he said softly.

He spoke the words, but he already knew the answer. He also felt sure he knew what Bob and Landon would tell him.

Then there was the other issue he needed to deal with: Lise Gentry. Whether he'd mention her this week was anybody's guess. Maybe next week after he got the time thing handled.

Yes, that was best. He never liked to air his dirty laundry, but dealing with two issues at once was something he just couldn't think to do right now.

Surely the guys would forgive him for holding back on that one.

The phone on his desk rang, and Ted reluctantly walked over to answer a call from a councilman regarding city business. The next call, which came immediately after the first, was a BTG Holdings contractor with an invoice that needed handling.

Sometime later, Ted realized he'd missed lunch and still had work to do. His stomach protested, but he ignored it.

Finally, a little before three, Ted set the phone down for the last time and grabbed his briefcase. He'd get nothing further done here today; that much was plain. Scooping up the drawings he needed, Ted stuffed them into the already crammed case and headed for the door.

"Hold my calls," he mouthed to his secretary, who held a phone against her ear.

"Wait," Bea called just before he escaped to the street. "I've got a message for you. Your dad called while you were on the line with that fellow from the inspector's office." She handed Ted the note. "Oh, and I saw Peach at the post office while I was out on my lunch hour."

"Is that so?"

Bea nodded. "We both agree you and that Texas gal make nice-looking sparring partners."

"I'm not even going to ask what you mean by that, Bea," he said as he stepped outside and allowed the door to close behind him. "Sparring partners, indeed."

And yet as he walked back to the truck that it seemed he'd only just left, Ted had his suspicions. In a town the size of Latagnier, nothing happened without witnesses. The question was which encounter with the aggravating architect had been seen.

Ted sped toward home, not liking the fact that it could have been any of several.

❧

Lise glanced up at the clock. A quarter past six and she was no closer to a solution to any of the multitude of problems facing her. Phoning Ryan loomed as a tempting solution, if not to talk through the issues, at least to complain about the unfairness. Only the knowledge that Ryan's answer would be to come and take over the project kept her from picking up the phone. Before she could call him, she would have to be prepared and know what she needed to do to get the project back on track.

Lise's thoughts wandered back a few hours to her parting words with the mayor. How dare Ted Breaux require her to come up with a new proposal! Of all the nerve.

She reached past the stack of memos and messages to lift the curling edges of the blueprint of the old bank that would become the new bookstore. How could she possibly improve on a solution that not only put money into the city's coffers but also resulted in the streamlined design that the tenant preferred?

"Impossible." And yet was it? She took another look.

Indeed, the millwork was a fine example of late-Victorian handiwork, and the cypress beneath the peeling paint bore none of the signs of aging that another wood might have. Perhaps it wasn't too late to do something else.

She rolled the plans and stuck them under her arm. It would be a long night, but she just might have an idea that could work. Her excitement at the challenge was only slightly tempered by the fact that she would be working on a solution that would make Ted Breaux happy.

And would prove him right.

Her cell phone rang. It was Susan.

"Hey," she said as she steeled herself for yet another conversation about why she would be missing Thanksgiving this year. "What's up, Susan?"

"I am underwhelmed by your enthusiasm, Lise," her older sister said.

"Sorry." The plans slipped and hit the floor. "I'm kind of in a crisis here. Can I call you back?"

"You can," Susan said, "but will you? You're not exactly the best at returning calls, as witnessed by the number of messages I've left over the past twenty-four hours." She paused, and her voice softened. "But then, I know you've got a lot on your mind."

"More than you know." Lise swung down to retrieve the

plans then tucked them back under her arm as she cradled the phone between her ear and shoulder. "I'm kind of dealing with a difficult situation here. Unexpected changes to the project at the last minute. And you wouldn't believe the guy who—"

Lise stopped herself. Any discussion of a single male with a pulse was likely to draw more than a little comment from her matchmaking sister.

"Well, suffice it to say the new mayor isn't making my life easy," she said. "I'll manage it, but the plans have changed, and the timeline is losing ground every day."

In the background, the sound of children's laughter rose then fell. The twins. Lise smiled despite her situation. Once she completed this project, she'd have to make more time in her life for the girls. They were growing so fast.

Susan's voice cut into her thoughts. "So I suppose it would be premature to ask if you've met the middleman yet."

"Um, yes," she said. "Extremely premature."

"All right." Her sister's sigh came through loud and clear, as did her disapproval. "But I wonder if all of this busyness isn't just a way of keeping your life at bay through work." Another pause. "Don't answer; just think about what I'm saying. We can talk about this another time."

"Thanks, Suse. Talk to you soon."

Lise hung up and tossed the phone into her purse lest her sister change her mind and continue talking. As she had the thought, she regretted it. Family was important; this she was only beginning to realize.

Perhaps in that one area she should be more like Ted Breaux.

But only in that area. Any other resemblance would be horrifying.

"Keeping my life at bay through work. I've never heard anything more ridiculous," she said as she wedged herself between the door and its frame to reach back and turn off the trailer's single overhead light.

Before she could clear the door and allow it to shut, her conscience got the better of her. Susan was right. She was awful at returning calls. Even worse at initiating them.

With a sigh, she caught the door and flipped the light back on. Setting her burden back on the desk, Lise fished for the phone and pressed the button that would place a call to her sister.

Time was not in her favor, and yet at that moment, it no longer mattered. The aggravation that was Ted Breaux faded as Susan's voice came over the phone.

Only one thought remained. How had she ever thought he was the middleman?

eleven

Ted scrubbed his chin with his palm and tried to keep his mouth shut while the noise of the Java Hut swirled around him. For the past fifteen minutes, Bob had been trying to diagnose Landon's troubles at home. Not that Landon was admitting he had them. Rather, the construction foreman was insistent that he had no idea what Bob was talking about.

He was a great husband. Always came home after work and never put his paycheck to use on anything but paying bills. He was a great dad. Always had time to let the kids know he cared. All of this Landon said with enthusiasm. Maybe a little too much enthusiasm.

And yet Ted hadn't heard a single thing in the way of behavior that supported those statements. It was enough to make him want to leave and go home. For all Landon's good intentions, his actions had yet to follow.

Of course, being the only member of this trio without a wife and kids to go home to, he was rarely consulted in these matters. What could he possibly know about life as a husband?

Ted watched Landon carefully while he sipped his coffee. At least Landon was no longer drinking. Ten months sober. That counted for something. And he'd stopped using the language he'd picked up in his previous life. Considering the colorful vocabulary the foreman brought to the job a year ago, this was another huge plus. Still, something wasn't quite right. Ted's instinct said it was exhaustion. Possibly insomnia, but likely just plain old mental fatigue.

He made a note to have Bea check on the last time Landon

took some vacation time. Maybe the guy just needed to get away.

But then, that was Ted's impression from the beginning. Finally, he could stand it no more.

"Look," Ted said as he set his coffee cup on the table with a bit too much force. "I know neither of you set much store in my opinion on this subject, what with me being the younger single guy, but it's easy to see what the problem is here."

Two surprised faces turned in his direction. Before either could express his astonishment, Ted held up his hands in his defense. "Okay, I know you're going to say that I don't have any frame of reference to diagnose marital troubles, but—"

"I don't have any marital troubles," Landon interjected.

"I wouldn't be so sure," Bob said. "Neecie certainly seemed to think there was something wrong when she told Bliss that—"

"Hey, I've got the floor here." Ted shook his head, being sure to keep his tone light. "Do you mind?" When neither responded, he continued. "So it's like this. When I'm up to my eyeballs in work and yet I know I'm supposed to be doing other things, those other things kind of lose priority. Like, for instance, I've been neglecting my time with God lately."

Ted paused to let that one soak in. He hadn't admitted that he'd lost his perspective and let that part of his life go because until now he hadn't seen the danger in it. Looking at Landon, seeing "tired" written all over his face, gave him pause to wonder if he, too, wore the same exhaustion.

If maybe this lack of resting in the Lord had seeped through into other things. Like his dealings with Lise Gentry. A pang of regret hit him, and Ted knew he should update his accountability partners on that situation, as well. For now, however, he decided to keep the subject to the topic at hand: Landon.

"Yeah, it starts out with that one time you decide you're too busy, and then one excuse becomes ten until the job is where you place your focus, and everything else, including God, has become a distant second." Ted shrugged. "I said you. What I meant is me."

Landon leaned back in his chair and toyed with his spoon. "So what are you saying, Ted?"

"I'm saying," Ted began, "that maybe just talking about being a great dad and husband isn't enough. I know I talk about spending time with God on a regular basis. I even put it on my calendar and set an alarm for it on my PDA. Do I do it? Not always. In fact, not nearly enough."

Bob warmed to the topic. "I know it's tough to keep life in balance. I struggle with it constantly. The temptation is there to do just one more thing at work before leaving for the day. Then after that, there's just one more thing, and then another. All the while I'm looking at the clock and justifying that I'm being productive, so what's the harm?"

Ted nodded. "Yeah, I know how that is."

Landon didn't move a muscle. Didn't even blink.

"Trouble is," Bob continued, "if I don't stop when my alarm goes off, I'm not going to be there in time for dinner. And we make dinner a don't-miss occasion." He gave Landon a hard look. "What's dinner like at your house?"

Landon thought a minute. "Kind of like a drive-through at a fast-food restaurant. With the kids in their various activities and Neecie working to make a go of the bridal shop, we don't sit down together much."

"You mentioned the kids and Neecie," Ted said. "Where are you in the picture?"

Landon sat up straighter. "Look, I'm trying hard to make up for the junk Neecie and the kids had to deal with while I was. . ."

"When you bailed on them?" Ted supplied. "Guess what?

You can't change it or make up for it. It is what it is. You just go forward."

"What are you, some psychiatrist now?" Landon shook his head. "You don't understand. I walked out on my wife and kids. Yeah, I fell off that oil rig, and legitimately I had some injuries, but when given the chance, I gave the nurses in that foreign hospital a fake name, and I walked away. And even before that, I wasn't exactly Father of the Year. Can you imagine not even remembering something as simple as one of your kids' birthdays or the difference in the time zone you're in and the one where your family lives?"

The hard, indifferent expression Landon had worn for most of their time together had slipped, and in its place seemed to be the face of a guy trying to come to grips with the pain he'd caused people he loved.

"This is old news," Bob said. "The past. What's the future?"

"You make it sound so easy. Just like that. I was but now I am. I was an idiot but now I'm not." Landon looked as if he was about to stand up and walk away. "I gave it all away," he finally said. "If I'm going to get it back, I've got to earn it."

"Did Neecie say that?" Bob asked. "Because she certainly hasn't indicated to Bliss as far as I know that she was putting you on some sort of probationary period. Last I heard, that woman was crazy about you."

The contractor let out a long breath then looked away. "She's crazy, all right. What she sees in me is beyond my understanding."

Ted laughed. "Yeah, mine, too, but who can understand a woman?"

"I can," Bob said, "and I can tell you there's one thing they want: time."

"Great," Landon said. "And I thought she wanted me to stop drinking, work in the same zip code as her, and provide for the family again."

"Come on, Landon," Ted said. "Those are givens. They're the minimum. Is that all Neecie's worth? Just the minimum?"

His friend thought a minute. "Maybe I've put her and the kids on the back burner to try to work off my penance." He shrugged. "But there's the hotel and that work we've bid on over in New Iberia. Face it," he said, "BTG is a success because we're so busy. What can I do, walk off the job? And if so, which job?"

"I've got an idea," Ted said. "What say we have Bob look over the books and see if we can't contract out more of the supervision? Not much, just some of it." Ted paused. "Maybe have someone take over the hotel renovations. The New Iberia work isn't slated to kick into high gear until after the first of the year, right?"

"Yeah," Landon said, "but we're in weekly meetings. Most of the time they're by conference call, but I've had to make a couple of trips out there to fact-find and to check up on some things. The closer it gets to breaking ground, the more I'll have to do that." He thought a moment. "But that's another six or eight weeks away at the soonest."

"All right. With someone else handling the hotel work, we could spare Landon, say, every other Friday until January. That ought to catch him up on about a fourth of the vacation time he hasn't taken over the last year and give him a couple of long weekends a month to do something with Neecie and the kids. What do the two of you think?"

Bob jumped in first. "That's a cosmetic job, the Bayou Place Hotel. Nothing structural, right?"

Landon nodded. "Anything along those lines has already been taken care of, but we can't leave it to the subs. Someone's got to stay on those guys, or I guarantee they'll start joking around and nothing will get done."

"Agreed." Bob looked to Ted then to Landon. "Can you think of a man on that crew who might be qualified to step up and take over?"

"I'd have to think on it a bit." He paused. "But a couple of names come to mind. The biggest issue on that site is watching the subs to be sure they're not tripping over one another or goofing around. They're good guys, but they just need to have someone occasionally remind them they're on the clock."

"Okay, good," Bob said. "That shouldn't be a hard job to fill, now that the big stuff is behind us. I'll run the numbers when I get back to the office in the morning." He downed the last of his coffee then set the cup back on the saucer. "I mentioned I use an alarm to get my rear out of the chair and into the truck heading home. I wonder if we might want to make that company policy."

"Company policy?" Ted frowned. "What do you mean?"

"I mean that when a man takes on the running of his own company, he generally starts with good intentions. I know we did. Taking care of our families, seeing that the city had the best we could offer. All of that is good stuff. Really good stuff." He paused to allow the waitress to clear their table. When she was gone, he continued. "But what I found out way back when I was running Tratelli Aviation and trying to raise Amy alone was that there rarely were enough hours in the day to do everything. All it took was to find someone to handle Amy, generally my folks, and I could work nonstop without giving a second thought to what day it was or whether my little girl remembered what her dad looked like."

Landon nodded while Ted kept silent. Only the dogs missed him when he worked half the night, and he wasn't completely sure about them. He could be replaced by a dog door and an automatic feeder in a heartbeat.

"One day I was complaining to my dad about all the things that were pressing in on me, and he asked me a question: Which was the most important eternally?"

"Meaning?" Landon asked.

"Meaning would the business deal I make or the paper-work I complete today have eternal rewards in heaven, or would I be better served by putting that deal or that paperwork off until tomorrow in order to go home and play with my kid? I might make a better business by staying, but I would certainly make a better kid by going." He waved for the check. "I don't want to preach, but it is interesting how things take on new importance when you weigh them on the eternal scale."

Ted let out a long breath. Bob hit the nail on the head. Anything he'd claimed important really wasn't when he looked at it this way.

"And now that Amy is grown, I can see how very fast time flies. I've made a promise not to let those times with the twins slip by like they did with Amy."

"So loving them isn't enough?" Landon said. "Working hard so Neecie doesn't have to isn't what I'm supposed to do?" He threw his napkin on the table. "I give up, then."

"No, don't give up." Ted gestured toward Bob. "I watched this guy sit right where you are and wonder how he was going to manage raising Amy when he was barely out of his teens himself, and I know you saw it, too."

Landon nodded.

"And I didn't always do such a great job," Bob said. "But I wanted to."

"Yeah, so do I," Landon admitted. "So you really think coming home for dinner and taking a vacation is the answer? It seems too simple."

"Simple? No way," Ted said. "It's going to be the hardest thing you've ever done. You're a hardworking man, Landon. One of the best contractors I've worked with on a job site."

"*One* of the best?" Landon joked. "Hey!"

"All right," Ted said. "The best—bar none. But that's your

problem. You're so good at what you do that you have a hard time turning it off and leaving for the day. Am I right?"

The look on Landon's face gave the answer he didn't vocalize.

"Okay, so you're going to make some changes." Bob gave Landon a playful jab. "I wonder what Neecie will say when you show up at the supper table tomorrow night."

Landon laughed. "She'll probably wonder who I am."

"So now about that vacation. Any idea where you'll go?"

"No. The kids aren't babies anymore, and they're all into their own things. I wouldn't have a clue where to start to plan something that would make them all happy."

"Talk to them," Ted said.

"Talk? Are you kidding?" Landon reached for his keys but made no move to leave. "If I didn't pull the headphones out of their ears, I'd probably never hear them speak, and I know they wouldn't hear me. As it is, I mostly get, 'Don't do that, Dad.' Unless they're out of money, of course."

"That's what kids do," Ted said. "I know I did."

"Me, too, but I'm glad now that my father didn't listen to my complaints. Teenagers may think they know everything, but once they have kids of their own, they're cured of it for sure."

"Is there something that you and the family used to enjoy?" Ted asked. "Something you all had fun doing in the past?"

A grin spread across Landon's face, followed by a chuckle as the waitress passed by to leave the check. "Yeah, there is one thing, but I don't see how they would appreciate it now. We used to go camping. You know, the kind of camping where you set up a tent and fish for your supper then clean it and cook it over an open fire."

Ted reached for his wallet and slapped a twenty down. "There's your answer. Take them camping."

"I will," Landon said with renewed enthusiasm. "It'll be

great. No iPods or cell phones or electronic whatchamacallits allowed. Just Neecie and the kids and me in the wilderness." He warmed to the topic. "I know we said I should take every other Friday off, but I wonder if I should take one week or two instead. You know, have some extended parent-child bonding time. I'm sure Neecie could find someone to cover for her at the shop if you two could manage without me."

"Well, yeah, we probably could." It was Ted's turn to laugh. "But judging from the fact these kids probably don't go without their electronics for longer than it takes to sleep at night, I'd suggest you go slow. Maybe a long weekend would be a good start."

"Yeah, no longer than four days, man. More than that and you're asking for trouble, in my opinion."

"You think?"

"I know," Bob said.

Ted nodded in agreement.

"All right, then." Landon rose and checked his watch then returned his attention to the table. "This is a great idea. Thanks. I'm going home to tell Neecie we've got plans for the weekend." He shook his head. "No, I'm going to surprise them all. Yeah, it'll be great. I think I'll head out to New Iberia and see what they've got over at the sporting goods store. If we're going to go camping, we're going to do this up right. New sleeping bags, new tents, the works."

He slapped Ted on the back and grinned at Bob. A moment later, his smile disappeared, and he ducked his head. When he looked up, his expression had turned serious. "I have to admit I was skeptical about joining you two. I figured sitting around every week and whining about my shortcomings wasn't exactly something I would look forward to."

"And now you do?" Bob joked. "Because I'm still getting used to whining about mine. Somehow it just doesn't come natural, even after all these years. Now Ted here, being a single guy, he's never had a problem with whining about his shortcomings. At least not that I've noticed."

Ted gave Bob a playful jab.

"Very funny," Landon said. "But truthfully, I do look forward to coming here. It's the dumbest thing, because I hate to talk about this stuff, but when I leave I'm always glad I have." He paused. "You don't judge me. You know where I've been and who I was, and you don't judge."

"How can we?" Ted rose to clasp his hand on Landon's shoulder. "The Bible says we've all fallen short. It's not about the fall; it's about the getting up and going forward again."

Landon shook his hand and then Bob's. A moment later, he headed out of the Java Hut with a smile on his face and a renewed purpose in his step.

"That went well," Ted said as he reached into his pocket for the truck keys.

"Sit down, Breaux," Bob said. "We're not done yet."

twelve

Lise's first stop after completing the call to Susan and dropping her things in the back of the SUV was the old bank building. The structure was a two-block walk, and she accomplished it at a brisk pace. With the sun now only a memory, the night's chill had begun to set in. She shrugged deeper into her jacket.

Still shivering, Lise rubbed her arms then reached into her purse for the small digital camera she was rarely without. With care, she documented each piece of millwork from every angle then stepped back to photograph the underside of the structure. Finally, Lise crossed the street and took a half dozen snaps of the entire facade.

Scrolling through the shots on her camera screen, she smiled. Although she would have to return and take more photographs in the daylight, the images Lise got were good enough for now. This visual combined with the measurements she'd taken on her first trip to Latagnier should serve her well in making the changes.

"*C'est bonne*, eh?"

Lise whirled around to see the source of the comment, a spry fellow of advanced years who promptly shoved his hand in her direction. Something about him seemed familiar, but that was impossible. The only citizens she'd met besides the contractors and crews, she could count on one hand. This man was neither.

"Oh, hello." Lise hurriedly turned off the camera and slipped it into her purse. "Yes, it is a beautiful building."

"You a reporter?" He gave her a sideways look. " 'Cause I

don't know you, and I know everyone from around here."

A truck approached, moving slowly then speeding up as it passed them. "What? Me?" she said, flustered. "No, hardly."

"Then you must be the lady architect. Peach told me all about you," he said as he shook her hand then stepped back seemingly to appraise her. Or perhaps he was looking past her at the building.

"Peach? Oh, the lady at the meeting." His puzzled expression let her know a more detailed explanation was needed. "I remember seeing someone named Peach at the September meeting at city hall. As I recall, she was expressing her opinion regarding the former mayor."

"Oh, *that* meeting. I'm sorry I missed it." The man chuckled. "And that'd surely be Peach. The Lord blessed her with a mighty strong set of opinions. Like as not, Harlon Dorsey didn't stand a chance."

It was Lise's turn to be amused. "He did seem a bit perplexed about how to handle her."

"I reckon that's been the experience of nearly every man who's had anything to do with her over the past fifty-odd years."

Another vehicle drove by, a small sedan with a backseat full of children. One of them waved, and Lise returned the gesture then looked at her watch. *Time to go. It's going to be a long night.*

"Well, I should be going," she said in what she hoped would be a firm but casual way. "It's been nice talking with you, sir."

The man leaned against the post and looked up at the ancient canopy of wood that covered them then ran his hand over the cracked and peeling paint. A piece of white paint flecked off and landed on his sleeve.

"I never get tired of looking at expert handiwork," he said, completely ignoring her statement as he swiped at the dried paint. "What about you?" His attention swung abruptly back to Lise as if he was waiting for her to argue or concur.

"Yes, it is beautiful," she finally said. "It's a pity the future tenant's asking for it to be removed. I'm hoping to strike a compromise."

"Is that so?" The man shook his head, and his thick mop of gray hair caught the breeze. "What sort of compromise?"

A thought occurred. Only two types of people would be admiring an old abandoned building this time of night: carpenters and kooks. From where she stood, he looked to be in the first category. At least she hoped he was.

"Do you know much about woodworking?"

His grin spread. "Oh, I know a fair amount, *cher*. Why do you ask?"

"This millwork is an authentic example of nineteenth-century craftsmanship. If I'm not mistaken, it's either heart pine or cypress."

Up ahead, the single working stoplight in Latagnier inexplicably turned from green to yellow and then to red. No car appeared, so Lise returned her attention to the carpenter, who was strangely quiet.

"Oh," he finally said as he rocked back on his heels, "it's definitely cypress. It's not nineteenth century, though. I'm sure of that."

"You think?"

"No," he said carefully. "I know this for sure. You don't believe me, eh?"

"Well," she responded, "the structure dates from the 1890s."

"Indeed it does, but the original didn't have anything to cover the door. Once the place changed hands, somewhere round '25 or '26, they got fancy and decided folks needed to have something to stand under when it rains."

"Really?"

"Really," he said. "That's when they called Ernest."

Lise ran her hand over the post. "I bet you're right." She warmed to the topic as she scratched at a spot of chipped paint with her thumbnail. "Look at that. It's still as nice as if the fellow who carved it just finished."

"Ernest."

She looked up to see that the man had moved closer and now studied the same piece of millwork. "I beg your pardon?"

"Ernest." He gestured to the carved wood. "The fellow who built this was named Ernest. Took him all of a month, I think."

"Really?"

"Yes, indeed. He used wood from the fix-up of an old schoolhouse, so in part you're right about it being nineteenth century. That's when the place was built. It started as a house and didn't become a school until the early 1900s. Maybe you've seen it?"

"The Latagnier School?" She'd read all about the historical designation of the old schoolhouse while doing research on the area. It, along with the bayou that ran nearby, had been on her list of places to visit.

The bayou. She sighed.

"That's the place," he said. "The folks in Baton Rouge came down and looked into putting a big plaque on the porch some years back so it would stay just like it was after the original Theo put it back together. Last I heard, the mayor was still working on finalizing that."

The mayor. Lise stifled a frown. "Yes. I've seen pictures of the place. Remarkable rural architecture."

"Rural architecture." He laughed long and loud. "That's a fancy description. You sure you're not a reporter?"

"I'm sure."

"All right," he said, a skeptical tone in his voice. "Well, pictures just don't do it justice. You really should get yourself out there to visit."

"I'll do that."

"Yes, well, the eldest son of the fellow who put the school-house back together is the man who did that work you're admiring."

"Well, how about that?"

He crossed his arms over his chest. "I'd be willing to venture a guess that the old boy would be proud to see his handiwork polished and put back the way he intended. That *is* what you're going to do, isn't it?" The man's eyes narrowed as he reached over to trace the wood grain on the porch post. "I'd hate to know this was going to be dismantled and shipped out to end up as some rich man's back porch."

For a second, her conscience pricked at the reminder of the original plans she'd made. "I admit it would go a long way toward defraying the city's costs for the renovation," she said in her defense. "If I can figure out a way to reduce the cost and keep the trim, I'll do it."

"Is that so?" He quit studying the post to offer a wink. "And what would you say if I told you I know a way to do both?"

"You're not serious." She paused, half hoping he would admit to the jest. "How?" she finally asked when he merely stared.

"Well, it's simple, really. First, you're going to have to find a man who knows enough about this sort of work to do right by restoring it but who won't charge you an arm and a leg to do it."

"Right," she said with a most unladylike snort. "No problem. I'll just snap my fingers and he'll appear."

"No need," the man said. "That's where I come in."

"You? I don't understand." Her hopes rose slightly, but so did her skepticism. What were the odds that the perfect man for this job would happen to show up just when she needed him? "You're a carpenter?"

"No." His phone rang, and he reached for it. "But I've got just the man for you. Hold on one second, Miss, uh. . ."

"Gentry. Lise Gentry."

He nodded then turned his attention to the ringing phone with a push of a button and a quick, "Hello," followed by "Hold on a minute."

The man pushed what she assumed to be the MUTE button. "How fast do you need this carpenter?"

"Yesterday," she said with a shrug. Her mentor's words came back strong and clear: *Always listen to the old-timers. They know all the best contractors.* "But I'll take him as soon as you can get him."

"Oh, I can get him sooner rather than later, but I'll have to take this call now."

Lise reached into her pocket, retrieved the business card case she always carried, and offered him a card. "That's my Houston address, but the phone number at the bottom is for the cell I have here in Latagnier."

He looked at the card but did not take it.

"Something wrong?" she asked.

"Oh no, cher. I don't need that card. I know where to find you." Another grin. "This is Latagnier. Everybody knows how to find everybody."

❧

"Hey, Pop," Ted said as he shifted the phone away from his ear and adjusted the hands-free earpiece. "Bea told me you called. Did I interrupt something?"

"Hello there, son. I didn't expect to hear from you so soon. Last I heard you were up to your eyeballs in some sort of city business."

"Was that Aunt Peach you were talking to?" he asked. "You could have called me back. Why don't you? I'll be home in a few minutes."

To his right, the marker indicating Breaux land appeared.

Through the trees, he could see the pastureland, the barn, and the clearing beyond. On the gentle rise at the back of the clearing sat the home he'd gladly traded his fast-track lifestyle for.

He thought of Wyatt and made a mental note to call him later. It had been too long since he'd spoken to his kid brother.

Not that communication was a strong suit among Breaux males.

"Peach?" His father's voice interrupted Ted's thoughts. "Oh no. Just a potential customer, but I'll know more about that in a day or two. Now where were we?"

Ted signaled to turn onto the stretch of blacktop the locals had come to call Breaux Road and felt the north wind rush in. Officially, the road was called Parish Road 712, but even the folks at the Latagnier post office would be hard-pressed to find it by that name.

"I don't know," Ted said as he slowed to wait out the leisurely pace of a local feline who seemed to be stalking one of the field mice that populated the nearby cane fields. "You called me, remember?"

"Oh yes. I was wondering how things were at the office."

"Office?" He pressed the button to close the window on the evening's chill then signaled to turn. The truck rolled onto Breaux land and began the trek toward the house. "Yours or mine?"

"Oh, mine," he said. "I hadn't spoken to you since the new tenant moved into your grandmother's house. Did she get settled in?"

The new tenant? The new thorn in his side was more like it. "I suppose," he said.

"That's a short answer."

Irritation flared. "There's nothing to tell." Ted sighed. "Sorry, Pop. It's just that the woman you rented the place to has turned out to be my worst nightmare."

Pop chuckled. "Is that so? She seemed so nice when I interviewed her by phone."

"*You* did the interview?" He eased around the tight turn at the edge of the converted barn and pointed the truck toward the parking space nearest the door. "I figured you'd delegated that to your secretary."

"Nah," he said. "This is your grandmother's house. I wanted to be sure to get someone in it who would take care of it."

"Is that so?"

"Out with it, son," his father said. "Something's eating at you, so you might as well just go on and say it."

Ted shifted into park and leaned back against the seat, suddenly exhausted. "All right, then." He paused to choose his words carefully. "You knew that woman was coming here to take the downtown renovation and yet you allowed her to move into Granny's house. How can you think that's a good idea?"

"Well, sure I did, Ted. Think about it. What better short-term tenant than someone who could likely rebuild the place if she had to?" he said. "And besides, if she skips on the rent, all I've got to do is look up her company in the city records and send 'em a bill. Made good business sense to me."

No, it didn't. Renting to the competition, signing an agreement with the person who robbed him of the project he was born to build, was bad business sense no matter how his father tried to justify it.

"Her boss spoke highly of her," Pop added. "If I were a suspicious man, I'd have to wonder why he was so enthusiastic."

"Oh, I can tell you why. If she's here, she won't be there." He frowned. "I'd give her a great reference, too, if it meant I could send her out of state for an extended period of time."

"Now, son."

"Sorry, Pop."

He really wasn't, but he was working on it. Lise Gentry belonged back in Texas. Of this much, he was certain.

Maybe he'd give this boss of hers a call. *Oh, what for? She's here. You're stuck with her.*

"Don't bother to try to convince me how sorry you are, son." He paused. "You're mad at me now, but when the checks don't bounce, you'll be glad I did this." His father's voice held more than a little defensiveness in it. But there was something more. For all the reasons against it, Pop sounded as though he was amused by the whole situation.

Ted unlatched his seat belt then opened the door. "What are you up to, Pop?"

"You think I'm up to something?"

Following the glow of the truck's headlights, Ted made his way to the door and shut it behind him then hit the button on his key chain and listened while the converted barn doors closed.

His truck safe for the night, Ted made his way to the back porch steps. "No, Pop, I don't *think* you're up to something. I *know* you are. I just don't know exactly what that something is."

"Now, son, you know me better than that."

Ted could imagine his father's face, a mask of innocence. Ted didn't buy it for a minute. Normally, his father would have been his staunchest supporter. What was it about this woman that turned even his father into mush?

"That is exactly the reason I'm asking." A thought occurred as he glanced down at his key chain. "And since when does the garage door opener for any of your properties go missing without a backup? You always leave a spare at the office and put the other in the garage of the property."

The hesitation in Pop's voice spoke volumes. "I'm not as young as I used to be," he finally said. "So maybe I forgot and put the remotes in the wrong file. Give an old man a break."

Old man?

Ted almost considered the scenario. Almost, but not quite. Ted Breaux III prided himself on his attention to detail. It was the hallmark of his career as a builder and the basis of the real estate business he'd developed since retiring.

And what he forgot, his secretary of thirty years remembered. Thus, nothing about the lost garage door opener made sense. Unless you factored in the possibility that his father was playing some sort of game with him.

Above all, he never, ever referred to himself as an old man.

"So about the reason I called today," Pop continued, interrupting Ted's thoughts. "I wonder if you're still interested in the property we talked about."

"I am." Ted turned the key and opened the door then braced himself as his furry security detail, a pair of one-year-old boxers, bounded toward him.

Pop laughed. "That was a fast answer."

"But not a fast decision." He paused to sidestep the dogs as they headed off the porch and into the yard, yipping like puppies and racing like the wind.

"Sounds like you just got home. How're Fred and Wilma?"

Ted laughed. "Right now they're running in circles and chasing bugs, so I'd say they're pretty happy."

"When you got those two, I knew for sure you were settling down. It's a good sign when a man does that, you know." Pop had only just begun to warm to the topic, and Ted knew it. His speeches on settling down were generally no less than ten minutes, often longer.

When Pop got started, there was nothing left to do but get comfortable. Ted settled on one of the old benches that Pop's uncle Ernest built back before the Depression and waited for the dogs to notice he'd joined them in the yard.

As expected, Ted listened politely and tried not to let his irritation show. It had been a long day. He reached for the tennis ball that Fred offered and gave it a toss; then he watched as Wilma followed her mate into the dark in search of the rolling treasure. If Pop was up to something that involved Lise Gentry, it would never work. Still, Ted would listen. This was, after all, his father.

When Pop was done, Ted offered to put steaks on the grill for dinner even though he was tired enough to settle for crackers and milk with a dash of Tabasco for flavor. He got the idea, however, that his father might want the company.

"Bring the paperwork and we'll get this deal done," Ted added. "That is, if you're sure."

"Oh, I'm sure."

"All right, then. See you in an hour."

Ted hung up and called the dogs. Once inside, he reached for the rib eyes he'd been saving for the weekend. It would be good to see Pop again. Somewhere along the way, the deal would be struck and he would own the home where the irritating architect now lived.

It might be a long night, however, if Pop started up again on the topic of settling down. The odds were with Ted, however. Pop rarely preached the same sermon twice in one day.

thirteen

Lise stifled a yawn as she drove into her parking place at the job site and shut off the engine. She'd worked into the night, but the result was a plan that she felt would make everyone involved happy.

Removing the millwork would be tricky, repairing and returning it to the facade trickier still. Thankfully, she had the old carpenter's phone number. Once she turned the plans in to the mayor's office, she would give him a call.

The thought of Mayor Breaux made her frown. "Stop that," she said under her breath. "You're not going to let that man get to you. Not today."

In truth, the day had dawned beautifully, and the brilliant blue sky promised it would continue. While the temperature was still on the frosty side, it had warmed a bit since yesterday. By midafternoon, she'd likely ditch her sweater and enjoy the sunny weather in her shirtsleeves.

That is, if she managed to get outside. Though today had long ago been set aside as a day to do paperwork, Lise was beginning to shuffle her calendar before she reached the door. Perhaps she could bring home the forms and memos and handle them after dinner.

Yes, if she did that, then she could give her attention to the work at the job site today. It would be good to pay a surprise visit while the contractors were on-site. Despite the fact that the job was now proceeding slightly ahead of schedule, she still saw far too many men dawdling and cracking jokes when they should be working.

In fact, just yesterday morning, she'd sent an e-mail to the contractor to let him know he needed to speak to his subs regarding this. Glancing around, she was pleased to see either no one had arrived or none loitered about.

Breathing a sigh, Lise turned the lock and stepped inside, trampling a slip of paper that someone had jammed under the door since her departure yesterday. She reached down to snag the paper then set it on her desk and allowed her purse and the blueprints to tumble after it.

As usual, the trailer's temperature hovered at frigid levels. She hit HIGH on the space heater and dragged it closer to her desk. If nothing else, her feet would be warm.

"This place certainly wasn't designed to accommodate women," she muttered. "At least not warm-blooded Southern women."

Lise landed in her chair with a less than ladylike plop. Then, with years of her mother's admonishments ringing in her ear, she straightened into a more ladylike position. Funny how she could remember little of her schooling before reaching the college level, even less of those classes that did not directly pertain to her life's passion of architecture. Yet words spoken to her well before puberty still bubbled to the surface when Lise committed such crimes as placing her elbows on the table during a meal or wearing white shoes after Labor Day.

She looked down at her scuffed steel-toed boots and smiled. They might be OSHA-approved regulation footwear, but they were definitely not Mother-approved.

"At least they're not white, Mother," she said under her breath as she eased the chair into position at the desk and shivered once more. "Now let's see what kind of fun I can have this morning." She glanced at that clock. A quarter to eight. "No sense making the trip down to city hall until after nine, so it looks like paperwork wins—at least for the next hour and fifteen minutes."

After that, she would pack this whole mess up and take it to the car. *I can handle it tonight at home.*

Home.

Strange that she would think of the little house next to the post office as home. And yet it already seemed much cozier and more welcoming than her place in Houston. In fact, were the cottage situated back in Texas, she might well consider living in it permanently.

Lise moved the blueprints aside, and a crumpled slip of paper fell into her lap. She set it atop the stack begging for her attention and flattened it with the palm of her hand.

It was a summons. To appear before the city council. To explain the impending bulldozing of the former hardware store.

"That's ridiculous. This was covered in the plans they approved two months ago." Lise let the paper drop onto her desk then snatched it back up. "Surely they don't intend to try to keep this from happening tomorrow."

She read it again. While the demand to appear was not signed by Ted Breaux, it was surely his handiwork.

Given the fact that her appointment with the city council was set for two mornings from now, it appeared the demolition would be postponed until after the issue was settled. Lise reached for her phone. The sub in charge of demolition would need to be notified. There was no sense paying the man to show up only to send him home.

Of course, if her amended plans were chosen, the possibility of demolition might not even exist. That would be settled once the mayor and council members took a look at the options.

A few minutes later, she'd made arrangements for the demolition crew to await her call on Monday. That gave the city council and their leader a full five days to get this handled and behind them. She dialed the number on the summons and left a message acknowledging receipt and promising to be there as requested.

Hanging up the phone, Lise briefly considered calling the office to get Ryan's take on the situation. It was likely he'd have some input that might be valuable. And yet he was the last person she wanted to speak to right now.

Well, he was a close second to Ted Breaux, anyway.

"All of that fuss about the millwork on the old bank was just a smoke screen to keep me occupied so I wouldn't be thinking about the demolition of the hardware store. He planned this." She took a deep breath and let it out slowly. "All right, then. If you want a fight, it's a fight you will have, Mayor Breaux."

Folding the summons, she stuck it into her briefcase and shook off her aggravation. If she had any hope of being successful in fighting this, she would have to focus. In order to focus, she must get her mind off Ted Breaux and his ridiculous attachment to the past. Tackling the mountain of paperwork she'd ignored last night was just the way to do it.

Lise opened the desk drawer to reach for a pen and froze. There among the disorganization that was her desk drawer sat a piece of printer paper. " 'Texas, don't mess with Latagnier,' " she read as she slammed the drawer shut.

Her hand shook as she leaned forward to rest her elbows on the desk. The first time she found a note like this, she'd ignored it. A prank, she'd decided, or something left over by the previous tenant.

But this time. . .

Lise opened the drawer a notch and peered at the page, one edge folded down and crumpled from her hasty move to shut the drawer. She looked for something to grab it with. The last thing she needed to do was tamper with the evidence.

"Who to call first, the police or the mayor?" she muttered as she snagged the corner of the page with a staple remover.

While the police could likely track down the culprit, Lise

could do it even faster. "The mayor it is."

Without bothering to take anything but her keys, Lise headed for city hall. If anyone was going to mess with Texas, then Texas would put a stop to it on her own.

Lise marched into the main lobby of the vintage 1960s one-story building that housed Latagnier's city government, police department, and water department. She clutched the staple remover and headed for the roster that would tell her where to find Ted Breaux.

The closest thing to the mayor's office was the city secretary, so she headed there instead. "Ted Breaux, please," she demanded of a woman whose eyes never left the cross-word puzzle she was working.

"Mr. Breaux's office is down the block."

"Down the block? Where, exactly?"

No response.

Lise sighed. Loudly. When the woman did not react, she did it again.

Finally, the woman looked up, peering at Lise over half-moon glasses that bore a cluster of rhinestones at each corner of the red frames. "He's down the block," she said in a voice thick with the local Acadian accent.

"Yes," Lise said, "I understood. What I don't know is exactly where down the block he is." Lise followed the woman's gaze to the paper she held at arm's length. "What?" she snapped.

"You looking to bring that to him, cher?"

"Yes, actually." Lise gave her a what's-wrong-with-that? look. "I'm just returning something he left at my office."

"Is that so?"

"Yes," she said a bit more tersely than she intended, "that *is* so. Now would you give me his address?" She took a deep breath and let it out slowly. "Please?"

"Which way you come here?" she asked. "From the left or the right?"

Lise had to think. "Um, the left. Why?"

"Then you walked right past it. You know that big old building with the sign that says BTG Holdings? That's where you gon' find the mayor."

She breathed a quick word of thanks and slipped out the door. The place was one she knew well, having followed Ted Breaux to the spot upon their first meeting.

The breeze had kicked up since she arrived at city hall, and holding on to the paper became more difficult. Finally, a gust ripped it from the staple remover's grasp and sent it spiraling into the street.

By the time Lise retrieved it, three cars and a UPS delivery truck had run over it. Giving up any pretense of hoping fingerprints might still be found, Lise nonetheless pinched the staple remover onto the edge of the page and held on tight.

The green awning proclaiming the offices of BTG Holdings and Ted Breaux, Architect, stood dead center of a redbrick building in the next block. The building was beautifully restored, likely at the hands of its tenant. A set of heavy doors slid open easily on brass hinges that looked as if they'd been polished this morning and opened onto a light-filled space with a carved staircase in its center.

A sign posted next to the brass and glass elevator stated that the BTG Holdings offices were up one flight of stairs. She stormed up them, taking the carpeted steps two at a time. By the time she reached the reception desk in the sparse but well-appointed lobby, Lise was out of breath.

A redhead of advanced years met her with a smile. Silhouetted by a set of French doors that opened onto a balcony and the trees beyond, the woman did not seem surprised to see her.

"Miss Gentry," she said as she bustled around the cherry-wood desk to clasp her free hand, "how nice to see you."

Lise frowned and gripped the staple remover to keep from dropping the paper again. "How do you know who I am?"

fourteen

"Everyone knows everyone in Latagnier." Her grin lit up her round face and made her blue eyes sparkle. "I'll just let Mr. Breaux know you're here," she said as she took a step back, seemingly to study Lise.

Lise shook her head, quickly uncomfortable under the woman's close scrutiny. "How did you know I came to see Mr. Breaux?"

"Oh, honey," the woman said, "it don't take Melba down at the city hall but two seconds to dial my number. Now getting her story out, well, that took a bit longer. Not much, but a bit nonetheless." She rose. "Anyway, you've got some sort of paper for the mayor, so let me just get him."

Lise breathed a sigh of relief. "Thank you."

"My pleasure." The woman took two steps toward a hallway that ran alongside her desk then cupped her hands around her mouth. "A visitor for you, Mr. Breaux," she called at high volume. "And, yes, it's someone you likely will want to see."

Silence.

"Mr. Breaux?" Pause. "Mayor?"

The ancient black phone on her desk rang. "Oh brother," the secretary muttered as she lunged for it. "BTG Holdings," she said in a prim and proper voice. "Bea speaking."

The sound of a man's voice could be heard both from the phone and down the hall. The words weren't clear, but the tone revealed obvious agitation.

"Well, of course I know how to use this silly phone," she said as she sat down. "If I didn't, would I be speaking to you now?" Bea looked up at Lise and rolled her eyes. "Yes, she can hear me." She held the phone away from her ear. "You *can* hear me, can't you, Miss Gentry?"

Lise nodded.

Bea returned her attention to the phone. "Yes, she can."

Again the voice drifted toward her. Again it sounded agitated.

"Well," Bea said, "it appears the resident architect cannot take a joke this morning."

She appeared to be waiting for a response from Lise. "I'm sorry," she finally said. "I do need to see him now, though; else I'd offer to come back at a more convenient time."

"Oh, honey, there's no need for that." Bea rose. "The mayor will see you now. Follow me."

Lise nodded and took a step back to allow the redhead to pass. The narrow hallway split the space in half, it seemed, with three doors on each side. Bypassing the first two, which were closed but bore brass nameplates that Lise had no time to read, she came to a halt outside the third. There in block letters engraved on an embellished brass nameplate were the words TED BREAUX IV, ARCHITECT.

Bea knocked then waited until the bear bade them to enter his cave. "Go on in," she told Lise, "but don't worry. I'm just outside."

"And likely listening to every word." Ted Breaux stepped into Lise's line of vision, blocking her view of his office. He gave her a cursory glance then stared at her hand and the paper dangling from the staple remover. "I'm extremely busy this morning. Is this something we can handle later, Miss Gentry?"

Is he serious? "No, Mayor Breaux, this needs to be handled now." She looked beyond him to the office. "May I come in, or would you prefer to handle this in the hallway?"

Lise looked over at Bea, who showed no desire to hide her interest in their conversation. Rather, she seemed quite enthralled.

The mayor noticed his secretary's presence and handled it by staring at her until she mumbled an excuse about running an errand and left. A moment later, the doors slammed behind her, and the office went silent.

"Come in," her host said, "and sit there." He gestured to one of two dark leather wing chairs. "Don't get comfortable. You won't be staying long."

"Fine." Lise pressed past him to settle in the spot he offered then watched him sit in the oversized desk chair. When he looked in her direction, Lise thrust the paper at him. "I'll only stay long enough to get an answer as to what sort of joke you think this is."

He took the paper, giving a quick look at the staple remover. "What's that for?"

"Minimizing the fingerprints," she said. "At least that was the original idea. Once the wind took it into the street and the cars ran over it, likely any fingerprints were lost. I still hope the police will be able to lift a few off there."

At her comment, the mayor let the page go, and it landed on the clean surface of his desk. "I fail to see what this has to do with me."

"Read it," she said.

"I did." He gave her an even stare. " 'Texas, don't mess with Latagnier.' So?"

"So?" She gave him what she hoped would be her best incredulous look. "So this isn't the first time I've found a letter like this in my office. In my desk, to be precise."

He shrugged. "Again, I fail to see what this has to do with me."

For a moment, she almost believed him. But this was Ted Breaux. The same person who opposed her very presence in Latagnier. The same person who told her to redo one perfectly good plan and scrap another. And those were just the first two projects he'd seen.

There was no telling how he would react when he read about phase two.

"Miss Gentry?"

She focused her attention on her host. "Yes?"

"Am I correct in assuming that you believe I may have had something to do with this?"

Lise looked into dark eyes that seemed to have no malice in them. "Well, I—actually. . ." Her courage returned, and along with it, the use of her voice. "Yes, actually, I did. You *are* one of the people in Latagnier who would like to see me gone. Can you deny that?"

The mayor shook his head. "Oh, you have no idea how much I would like to see you gone," he said. "However, I had nothing to do with this letter. It's a bit dramatic and juvenile, don't you think?"

Two of the very words she might have used to describe Ted Breaux.

"You don't believe me?" His dark brows rose. "Honestly?"

Her resolve slipped. The man did look as though he might be telling the truth. He certainly managed to give the impression that he took great offense at her accusation.

Lise shifted positions. With the sun streaming through the windows overlooking Latagnier's main street, the office took on a warm glow. Except for such modern conveniences as a laptop, a pair of telephones, and a stereo receiver with a red iPod plugged into its center, the room could have taken her back in time at least a hundred years. The desk had to be mid-nineteenth-century and the chair a good copy of one from the same vintage. A pair of bookcases and a drafting table made of what looked to be cypress guarded the opposite wall.

"What you're not considering," he said slowly, "is that there were a whole bunch of people at that meeting two months ago who cheered for me and booed for Mayor Dorsey. Those are the people who got me elected, and those same people are the ones who agree with what I stand for."

"And one of the things you stand for is to avoid change at any cost."

The mayor looked as though he intended to argue the point then thought better of it. "All right," he said slowly, "let's start from the beginning. Are you in fear of any harm coming to you?"

"Harm?" She hadn't considered that the letters could be a warning of something worse to come. Rather, Lise had figured she was being either teased or tormented. Either was harmless except for the disruption and irritation it caused.

"Yes, harm." The mayor steepled his fingers and peered at her as if waiting for a petulant child. "Do you feel unsafe in Latagnier?"

"No," she said. "I'm just. . ." Lise chose her words carefully. "I'm tired of being toyed with. Whatever creep is responsible for sneaking into my trailer and planting these in my desk needs to be caught and punished."

"Agreed." He glanced down at the page then back up at Lise. "Did you lock your office door last night?"

"Of course I did. I'm not irresponsible, you know." The moment the harsh words were out, she longed to reel them back in. "I'm sorry. That was rude. I'm just, well, preoccupied."

He seemed as though he might be waiting for her to elaborate. She did not.

"Yes, well, I can see how this would be distressing to you. Anyone else have a key to the office?" When she shook her head, he continued. "All right, then that leaves one of two possibilities. Either someone has come in during office hours and stuck it there when you weren't looking or someone's getting into the trailer at night."

"I can guarantee it's not the first one; at least I'm fairly sure I can. I don't think it was there when I left last night."

The mayor frowned. "Then we're going to have to do

something about this." He pressed a button on the phone console then lifted the receiver to his ear. "Bea, would you get me the chief on the phone?"

The chief? As in chief of police? Obviously, whoever had been playing tricks on her was not Ted Breaux. Getting the police involved was a sure clue.

He set the phone back in its cradle. "I think we're going to have to move your office until this is figured out."

"Move the office?" While she wouldn't be sorry to leave the cold-as-an-icebox trailer, she did wonder what sort of accommodations she would be moving to. "Do you really think this is necessary?"

"I do." His gaze met hers. "And since we will be working closely together on this project, I think it would be best for you to take one of the empty offices in this building."

"Oh, no way," Lise said. "I can't do that," she amended. "I'm sure you're much too busy to have me and all my subs coming in and out."

The mayor drummed his fingers on the desk and looked as if he might be considering her statement. He opened his mouth to respond, and then the phone rang.

"Thank you, Bea," he said. "Put him through."

In under two minutes, Ted Breaux had relayed Lise's situation to the police chief. While the men chatted about possible solutions, Lise basked in the warmth of the sunshine streaming through the mullioned windows. It would be nice to work in such luxury.

Except for the fact that she'd be sharing an office with Ted Breaux. Well, not an office, exactly, but she'd be right down the hall.

You've done it before. Lise lifted her gaze to the tin ceiling and the original converted gaslight fixture. *This would be no different than all those months you spent working in close proximity to Ryan.*

Lise turned her attention to the mayor, who now jotted a phone number onto a legal pad already half filled with doodles and notes. "Just for now," she heard him tell the chief. "Until whoever this is trips up."

He concluded the call and set the phone down then began scribbling something on the pad. Lise could have easily snooped and read the mayor's handiwork. From childhood, she'd learned to read just as well upside down as right side up.

"All right," he said. "I've got to get Bea busy on having the office furniture brought up from storage. I'm sure she'll find someone to handle that by tomorrow or the next day."

"I'm on it," Bea called from the hallway. "Consider it done."

He stifled the grin tugging at the corners of his mouth. "Okay, that's one thing I don't have to warn you about. Working here means you're working with Bea, and she's, well, a bit eccentric."

"I heard that," drifted toward them from somewhere beyond the open door.

"She also believes that shameless eavesdropping is perfectly all right." He paused and waited while the outer door shut. "That gets her every time," he said with a shake of his head. "Don't let her fool you. Bea's the best. Whatever you need done, she'll do."

"Including eliminating the obstacle to progress also known as the mayor of Latagnier?"

What she meant as a joke fell sadly flat. He was an obstacle to progress. She'd not apologize for that, even if she might have been better served not to mention it.

"Look, maybe this office-sharing thing is a bad idea. I know I can work just fine at home. Maybe that's what I need to do until things settle down." She rose. "Yes, that's it. I'll just do that."

"Sit down, please," he said. "Do you really want subs tromping through your house?" He paused. "My house."

"Your house?" She complied with his request to sit, but only because she felt her knees go weak and her legs begin to wobble. "What do you mean, your house?"

His smile was glorious, his face a mask of merriment. It was the first time Lise had seen the man genuinely happy since they stood ordering double dark chocolate caramel ice cream with red hots.

"What I mean is, the home where you live is now mine." He paused, obviously to let the information soak in slowly. "It was my grandmother's. When she passed on, it became my father's. Now, at least once the paperwork is complete, it will belong to me."

Could the news get any worse? First, Ted Breaux's father was her landlord, and now the place was changing hands so that Ted Breaux himself would own it?

Lise closed her eyes and let out a long breath. This was too much for one day, especially a day that had begun only a few hours after the previous one ended.

"You know what?" Lise said. "Congratulations on your foray into the real estate market."

The statement did its intended job. Latagnier's mayor looked stunned. "Thank you," he finally said.

This time when Lise rose, she did it without warning and with the intention of ignoring any demands to take her seat again. "I assume you will honor the lease your father signed with me," she managed with what little dignity she had left.

"Of course," he said.

"Good. Then I'm going to go back to the trailer and get my things. Will you have Bea call me when my office is ready?"

"Yes." He stood and made his way around the desk then reached for his jacket. "Let's go."

"Where are *we* going?"

He shrugged. "The chief asked me to stick close to you until the case is solved. That especially means not allowing you to go back into the crime scene alone."

Crime scene? Sure, she felt uncomfortable about the note, but quarantining the trailer and calling it a crime scene was a bit much. When she told him that, he ignored her.

"After you," he said as he opened the door.

"Do I have a choice?" she muttered.

"I heard that," the mayor said, "and the answer is no."

fifteen

When they arrived at the trailer, a cruiser marked with the logo of the Latagnier Police Department greeted them out front. The door to the trailer had been propped open, leaving Lise to wonder how the overly large officer had gained entry so easily.

Of course, a man the size of Officer Thibodeaux probably could have lifted the thing off its hinges if he so desired.

After asking a few questions, the officer allowed Lise to gather up the things she would need for the next few days. The mayor made a call, and someone from his office arrived a few minutes later with a stack of boxes. In short order, her files and paperwork had been packed and transferred to the BTG Holdings office down the street.

"If there's anything else we need, the chief or I will call you," Officer Thibodeaux said.

Lise reached for her purse to retrieve a business card. "Here," she said. "It's my Houston address, but the phone number's the cell I have with me here."

The policeman looked up from the clipboard where he was taking notes. "Don't need it."

"But how will you find me?"

He stared past Lise to exchange a bemused look with the mayor. "This is Latagnier."

On another day, she might have found the statement amusing. "Yes, right," she said without further comment. "If that's all you need, then I guess it's time to go."

"We'll catch him, ma'am," the officer said. "There's not much that happens in Latagnier, so you can be assured we're going to put everything the department's got on the case."

Everything they've got? Dare she guess how little the Latagnier Police Department had in the way of crime-fighting tools?

"Thank you," she managed before turning toward the door. "In the meantime, are there any precautions I should take?"

"Honestly, Miss Gentry, this is probably nothing." He scratched at his scalp with his pen. "Likely somebody's trying to send a message about what they think of your work here. There are a lot of people who figure Ted here should have got that job."

Lise sighed.

"Be that as it may," he continued, "just watch your back and be aware of what's going on around you. The chief says you're moving in over at Ted's place."

"I'm borrowing one of his offices for a day or two," she quickly clarified.

"Yeah, well, I think that's wise. You got someone staying with you at night?" This time the officer looked to the mayor for the answer.

"I'll be fine," she said before he could speak for her. "After all, this is Latagnier, right?"

A grin spread across the officer's broad face. "It is at that, ma'am. You've got a point." He went back to his work, dismissing them as he turned to inspect the contents of the desk drawer.

"You look tired," the mayor said as they walked out of the trailer into the early afternoon sun. "And I'm guessing you haven't had anything to eat since breakfast."

"Ah," she said. "Then you'd be wrong."

He sidestepped the narrow walkway to allow her to pass. "Oh?"

She nodded. "I slept through the alarm and forgot to grab breakfast."

"That settles it, then." He gestured to her SUV still parked near the trailer. "Go ahead and bring your car down to our parking lot and find a place to park there. I've got something back at the office that'll hit the spot."

Lise took two steps toward her vehicle then stopped short and whirled around to stare at Ted Breaux. "Why are you doing this?"

"Doing what?"

"Being nice." She shook her head, exhaustion pressing hard now. "Why?"

He quirked a dark brow. "Are you under the impression that I have some ulterior motive for moving you over to my building? That would be ludicrous. We don't even like each other."

The statement stung despite the truth in it. "Exactly," she said. "So again, I have to wonder why you're being so nice. What in the world are you thinking?"

"I'm thinking it's the least I can do." The mayor shrugged. "Because it's likely my fault this is happening to you."

Lise froze, barely breathing as her eyes narrowed. So it was as she expected. Ted Breaux had planned this. She chose her words as carefully as she could, keeping in mind the officer was just inside the door.

"Explain that statement."

"In case you've missed it, I haven't exactly been your biggest supporter."

His wry laugh almost made her smile in spite of herself.

"Yes, I did notice something like that."

"Well," he said as he raked his hand through his hair, "my guess is that I may have stirred up a little too much enthusiasm for my cause with some of my constituents."

"I see." She glanced around then returned her attention to the mayor. "Any idea who this overly enthusiastic constituent might be?"

He looked offended. "If I did, don't you think I would have told the police?"

"Maybe," she said slowly. "But then again, maybe not."

❧

Obviously, insanity ran in his family. Starting with his generation. Specifically with him.

Ted stared at the woman in front of him and bit back a sharp response. *Would the real Lise Gentry please stand up?* From snippy to sweet and back again in nothing flat.

He took a deep breath, let it out slowly, and prayed for patience. "Miss Gentry," he said, "I assure you the last time I decided to withhold evidence in a police investigation, I was ten and my brother, Wyatt, and I were playing cops and robbers."

Lise looked at him as if he'd grown a second nose. "I've never met a man who made less sense than you," she said, "although I was once closely acquainted with one who came in a close second."

This conversation was going nowhere, and it looked as though the investigation had moved from inside the trailer to outside. If the boys in blue were correct, he'd have the lady architect out of his office before the weekend.

Ted let out a long breath. Today was Wednesday. He could do this.

The object of his thoughts held her keys in her hand and seemed to be waiting for a response. If only he'd paid better attention to what she'd said. Something about an acquaintance of hers. It was all a bit too much to deal with.

Maybe he'd have to take a couple of days off while Lise Gentry was in the vicinity.

She was still staring. An answer was obviously still expected.

"Just move the car so Tiny can finish up his work here," he said as he turned on his heels and strode across the parking lot. He'd feed her then leave. That would make up for his bad behavior and keep him from losing his mind at the same time.

And the dogs would be thrilled. Maybe he'd take them down to the bayou and let them run there. They always liked it when he did that.

"Tiny?" he heard her say with a chuckle that held no humor. "Honestly?"

"Did you call me?" Officer Tiny Thibodeaux asked.

"Never mind," the woman called.

Ted heard the car start then listened as the tires crunched the gravel as they rolled toward him. For a brief moment, he wondered if it would be safer to walk on the curb away from the path of the fancy SUV and the irritating woman at the wheel.

"Want a ride?" she asked as she came to a stop beside him.

"Thanks, but no." He jogged across the sidewalk and dodged an oncoming truck to reach the other side of the street. "I prefer to walk," he added as he set out toward the office. He punched in the number for Bea and gave her instructions then tucked the phone back into his pocket.

She was right about one thing, he'd decided by the time he arrived on his doorstep. What in the world was he thinking? He didn't even like her.

Still, he knew he had plenty of penance to do for the way he'd treated her. Bob's warning at their last accountability meeting chased him back to the office. His friend had nailed him on two key points: making quiet time a priority and getting along with Lise Gentry.

While he'd easily cleared his schedule to make time for the Lord each morning, the other issue still gave him trouble. Funny how the two had become intertwined since Bob pointed them out. Often a great deal of his prayer time was spent asking the Lord to help him with the issue of Latagnier's lady architect.

When he reached the office, Lise Gentry was waiting in the foyer. She fell in behind him as he headed upstairs.

"We're all on a first-name basis here. Put your things in the first office on the left," he said. "That will put you within earshot of Bea but out of her line of sight." He shrugged. "That's the best I can do. Bea's going to know everything that's going on in here anyway, but at least you won't have to look up and see her watching you."

"That's just creepy, Ted."

He laughed. "Nah, it's really not. Bea's great. She just needs a little more to do."

"I heard that." Bea stepped out of a room at the end of the hall. "And thank you, boss. I think you're great, too."

"Great, Bea. Now you'll be asking for a raise."

"Oh no, hon," she said as she made her way back to her desk to catch a ringing phone. "You all can't pay me what I'm worth anyway, so why bother trying?"

"On that note," Ted said, "put your things in the office and meet me in the kitchen. If you have any question on where it is, follow your nose."

"That smells delicious," Lise said as she stepped into the empty office then came back out. "What is it?"

"Shrimp gumbo." Ted turned the corner. "I keep some in the freezer for emergencies."

"Wonderful." She pulled out a chair and sat down. "I haven't had gumbo in ages. As I recall, I really liked it."

"Liked it?" He laughed, and for a moment their differences dissolved. Bea had already seen to the details. All he had to do was dish up the rice then ladle gumbo atop it. With a flourish he added filé—an essential garnish made from dried sassafras leaves—and the food was ready.

"Miss Gentry," he said as he set the bowl before her then handed her a spoon, "you have never had my gumbo. Prepare to fall in love."

Ted sat across from her and watched while the Texan had her first bite of real Louisiana shrimp gumbo.

"Oh," she said as she dipped her spoon in for more. "This is amazing."

"Mm-hmm," he said. "At least you've got good sense where food is concerned."

"I'm not going to ask for clarification on that statement," she said. "Although I'm sure this disappoints you."

"Me? Disappointed?" He snapped his fingers and headed for the fridge. "Oh, wait. I forgot the best part. Hold that bite."

Lise froze, her spoon held midway to her mouth. "I refuse to believe anything can make this taste better."

"Try this." He uncapped the Tabasco sauce and doused his gumbo then put a few drops in hers. "Stir it up and see what you think."

She did as he asked then tasted it. "Not bad," she said.

"Not bad?" His pride wounded, Ted set the Tabasco on the table between them. "Just 'not bad'?"

Lise eyed his gumbo bowl then turned her attention to the container of Tabasco. "I think I know what it needs." While he watched, she squirted a liberal amount of the fiery substance into her bowl. "There. That ought to do it."

"Hey," he said, "you might want to watch that stuff. It's hot."

Too late. Ted waited for the gasp, for the tears in her eyes and the frantic search for anything liquid that marked a rookie to the wonders of Tabasco.

Instead, she swallowed, smiled, and reached for another spoonful. Had Lise Gentry not been his opponent in business and his nemesis in life, she might have earned more than just his respect at that moment.

Grown men had walked away from fiery concoctions much less potent than the one she couldn't seem to stop eating. He picked up his spoon.

"I can't help but notice the cornice moulding in here." She lifted her gaze to the twelve-foot ceiling. "Did you restore it or have it made? I don't think I've ever seen such quality. Much better than what I've seen in the rest of this suite."

"Actually, we carved this room out of warehouse space, so I had to copy what was already here." Ted took a bite of gumbo then set his spoon down.

"You did this?" Her gaze collided with his, and something odd took flame inside him. Something that could not be contributed to the Tabasco.

"Yeah," he said. "It was kind of fun, actually, but then, I love a challenge."

The spark in her eyes fanned the flame. "Amazing," she said under her breath. "Absolutely amazing."

And all he could say was a soft, hopefully inaudible, "Yeah."

Watch yourself, Breaux. This is one interesting woman.

Ted pretended to lose himself in the experience of dining while covertly studying the lady architect. In between bites of gumbo, she continued to study his handiwork in the room with what was obviously an appreciative eye. Each time something Lise saw caused the slightest hint of a smile, the flame grew.

"Thank you for lunch," she said as she set her spoon into the empty bowl and made to rise. "I should let you get back to whatever it is you do around here."

"Not yet," Bea called. "I've got dessert in the freezer."

They shared a laugh.

"How did she hear that?" Lise asked.

Ted leaned close, his tone conspiratorial. "I have a theory. Somewhere along the way, she conned one of our sub-contractors into setting up an elaborate secret eavesdropping system in the building. It's likely the controls are in that huge purse she carries."

Lise nodded. "Good to know," she said.

"I hate to disappoint her," Ted said. "Should we see what

she's got for us in the freezer?"

She seemed to be considering the question. "Sure," she finally said, "but I wonder if we might talk some shop over dessert."

Warning bells went off in his head. "Talking shop" with Lise Gentry generally did not end well. "I suppose that would be all right." Ted stood and cleared the table then reached for a dish towel to clean off the surface.

Her nervous look did not lessen when she returned with a roll of documents. As she set them on the table between them, she cast a glance in his direction. "I did what you asked."

"What I asked?" Ted moved toward the freezer, his eyes still on the document.

"The millwork on the old bank. I figured out how to save it." She lifted her gaze to meet his, still looking unsure. "You were right," she added in a voice so soft that even Bea and her supersonic hearing would have missed.

Inexplicably, at that moment the flame became a full-fledged inferno, and Ted Breaux figured out why the woman of his nightmares just might possibly be the woman of his dreams, as well.

He nearly dropped the ice cream dishes. That was it. He'd surely lost his mind. And it was all Lise Gentry's fault.

"Here," he said as he set the frozen bowl in front of her. "Now show me what you've done."

Lise glanced at the ice cream and smiled. "Is that what I think it is? Double dark chocolate caramel with red hots mixed in from the Dip Cone?"

"Yes," Bea said from the outer office.

"Thank you," Lise called before turning her attention to the plans. "I'm not saying my plan wasn't the best for the city, but I have come up with one that I think you will like."

For the next ten minutes, Lise outlined her plans in between bites of ice cream. By the time she was done, she'd shown him not only how the millwork would remain on the old bank but how they could feasibly keep the hardware store's outer structure intact while gutting the interior and repurposing the space.

Much as he hated to admit it, her plans were better than anything he'd come up with thus far. He met her stare. "And you did all of this last night?"

"And this morning."

"It's. . ." Could he say it? "Well, what I mean is. . ." Dare he say the words? "Wow," was all he could finally manage.

"Wow?" A wrinkle creased her forehead as she frowned. "Is that a good 'wow' or a bad 'wow'? There are two kinds, you know."

Ted set aside his ice cream spoon and rose, rounding the table to join her. They stood side by side, shoulder to shoulder, the plans unfolded on the table before them.

"I have a couple of questions," he said.

"Of course." Her voice was soft, her breath scented with chocolate and cinnamon.

Somehow Ted managed to ask all the questions but one: *What has come over me?* That one he kept to himself.

"Well?" she said, and he realized he'd been staring—at her.

"Well," Ted repeated, "I'm favorably impressed. This is very close to what I'd hoped you would come up with."

Liar.

"That is—what I meant to say is. . ." Ted swallowed hard to clear his suddenly dry throat. "You've gone over and above what I'd hoped. You've. . ." Again he had difficulty speaking. He turned toward her. "You've captured it, Lise," he finally said. "I think this is the plan that will save Latagnier."

"Do you think so?" Her lips turned up in a shy smile. "There are certainly more options than the ones I've presented here."

"No." Ted said the word more sharply than he intended. "No," he amended in a softer tone. "This is. . ." The inferno raged. "Just perfect."

"There is one more thought," she said slowly. "It involves the downtown streets. They're cobblestone and quite lovely."

"Lovely," he echoed, but his mind was not on bricks.

For a second, Ted thought she might have sensed his distraction. Then she continued. "I had a thought that maybe," she said, "and this is a *huge* maybe, but what do you think of the idea that the city close two blocks of downtown between the bank and the hardware store to vehicles and make it a pedestrian mall? They've done a great job of this at the Third Street Promenade in Santa Monica, and given the light traffic, I think it might work well here."

Ted tore his attention away from the architect and focused on her drawings. "Show me what you mean."

Lise leaned forward and began to point out the features of her plan. Ted, however, was more intent on trying to keep his eyes off her.

When had the aggravating woman grown so pretty? He followed her gaze then found his attention splintered.

She looked up abruptly, eyes wide. "There's just one problem."

He leaned closer. "Just one?"

Lise nodded. "I wonder if you would present this to the city council. Considering the fact that you're their mayor and I'm the stranger, I think the idea would probably be better received if it came from you."

Ted frowned. "But you need to get credit for this. It's a brilliant plan, and it's important people know you thought of it."

Lise reached out to touch his sleeve, a gesture both innocent and enticing. "No," she said softly. "What's important is that Latagnier gets the downtown it deserves. If that happens because you tell them about it instead of me, who cares?"

I care. The knowledge stunned him. So did his desire to kiss Lise Gentry. Before he could act on it, he made his excuses and fled.

sixteen

"I'm an idiot." Ted pushed back from the table and threw his napkin onto his plate. "A total idiot."

In an uncharacteristic move, Ted had asked that Bob and Landon meet him at his place for their weekly meeting. What he had to admit didn't need to go any farther than the two of them, and one never knew when something might be overheard in town.

With Fred and Wilma snoozing in the sun, their bellies full, silence reigned. The day was glorious, one of those crisp afternoons when the sunshine made the temperature just right for being outdoors. And any day outdoors was a good day for grilling.

Ted inhaled the tangy scent of mesquite that still hung in the air around them then let out a long breath. Life truly was good, even if he was an idiot.

"So you're an idiot." Landon reached for another rib eye and placed it on his plate before looking over at Ted. "Care to be specific?"

"I almost kissed the woman, Landon. Did you not hear me when I told you what almost happened in the break room at work?"

"Yeah." Landon chuckled. "What do you think, Bob?"

Bob stretched his legs out and leaned back against the chair. "Yep, I think he's an idiot." He laughed. "But probably not for the reason you think."

"Oh, come on. I almost kissed a woman I can barely tolerate. Why, the idea of her just sets me to. . ." He paused. "Why are the two of you staring at me?"

His friends exchanged one of those we-know-something-you-don't looks.

"Okay, spill it, Bob," he said.

Bob sat up straight and stared at Ted. "All right, but you're not going to like it. Remember when I called you on your lack of time for the Lord?"

"Yeah."

"And remember when you said you were going to be praying about how to handle this thing with the woman who got the job you wanted?"

Ted was growing impatient. "Yeah," he said. "But I fail to see how the two are connected. They're different—"

Bob held up his hand to silence him. "Don't you see? The minute you decide to spend more time with God, you choose her as your first topic of conversation."

"Yeah." He looked to Landon for support but found none. "What of it?"

"I'm curious. Did you give God any instructions on how you felt He ought to handle this gal?"

Spoken like a man who already knew the answer. "I might have mentioned a thing or two about it," was all Ted would admit. His penchant for making plans and asking God to bless them was an ongoing struggle.

This time, however, he had no real plan for the situation except to get his way. But then, wasn't that the universal plan?

What he'd asked, in actuality, was to see the lady architect come to agree with him on the way the project should go. As Lise Gentry wore on him, Ted had also made mention of sweetening her temperament and keeping her near so he'd have some idea of what she'd do next so he could be prepared.

He turned his attention back to Bob. From the looks on his friends' faces, his expression gave away his answer.

"Did He answer?" Bob asked.

Ted could only nod.

"Then you're an idiot."

❧

It was a conspiracy, Lise decided as Monday rolled around, and every member of Latagnier's city government was in on it. Lise had been an unwilling freeloader on Ted Breaux for several days now, and she was nowhere closer to being allowed back into the trailer that had served as her office.

While she enjoyed the comfort of working from a lovely office and especially liked having Bea to talk to, the proximity to Ted Breaux was beginning to wear on her nerves. The situation was far too close to the one she'd endured back in Houston with Ryan. Unlike Ryan, however, Ted Breaux seemed to be out of the office more than he was in. This was both a relief and a source of irritation.

How did the man expect to be considered a businessman if he didn't keep business hours? And how was she going to get him out of her mind if every time someone walked down the hall, she expected it to be him?

Why, she'd even begun to think there might be hope for him as a middleman after all. It was a long shot, but one she might be willing to take.

Not that she ever expected him to show any interest. He'd certainly done his best to avoid her all week. That alone spoke volumes.

The phone rang in the outer office, and Lise jumped. She'd been dodging Ryan's calls since last week, and over the weekend he'd become more insistent that she answer. By last night, she'd turned off her phone.

It was halfway through Monday morning, though, and time to turn it back on. As she did, the messages rolled across the screen. Ryan. Ryan. Ryan. Ryan.

The list went on, all spelling out an ultimatum: Call Ryan.

She pushed the phone away and glanced at her calendar.

With the change in circumstances came a postponement of all major stages of the project, including Ted's meeting with the city council.

It was frustrating, to say the least. So were the strange feelings she got every time she thought about that lunch in the break room last week. For a moment, it seemed as though the man might have actually been planning to kiss her.

A part of her found that notion absolutely revolting, seeing as the two had a less-than-pleasant past. Another part of her—a much larger part—however, got tingles whenever she considered it.

"Telephone, Miss Gentry. Line two."

Lise smiled. "Thank you, Bea." She pressed the button to activate line two and was greeted by the cheerful voice of Ryan Jennings.

"Ryan," she said. "How did you find me?"

"I have my ways." His laughter translated as cold and not the least bit cheerful. "I've felt a little ignored, Lise. Any reason you're not calling me back?"

"No," she said, "except that I don't work weekends."

"I'm hurt," he said, but she knew he didn't mean it. Ryan was the Teflon Man. Nothing stuck. "But I'll live." He paused. "We need to talk about the funeral home."

"About that." Lise's attention strayed to the window, where a pair of squirrels tussled on the sill. "I've had a chance to study the demographic here, and I'm not certain there's support for that kind of store."

"Well, that's fine, because I've got another client who outbid them. Tell me," he said slowly, "do these people eat?"

"Well, of course."

"And do you figure they like Cajun food?"

"Come on, Ryan," Lise said. "You're wasting my time with the games. Just tell me what we're turning the funeral home into and I'll start on the changes to the plan."

"A Cajun-themed restaurant."

"Really?" She thought a moment before allowing her grin to grow. "Yes," she said, "that would work quite well with the tweaks Ted and I have made to the promenade."

"Tweaks? Promenade?" She could hear him sputtering. "And who is Ted?"

"Ted is the mayor of Latagnier. Ted Breaux. Surely you remember, although you certainly forgot to warn me."

Ryan laughed. "Oh yes, I remember now. Is he giving you any trouble?"

"Only when I think about him," she muttered. "Tell me about the restaurant," she said before he could ask her anything further.

Lise scribbled notes as fast as she could, and yet she could barely keep up with Ryan and his ideas. By the time she hung up, she had a full page in front of her.

"What's up?" Ted asked, and she jumped.

"I didn't see you standing there." She motioned for him to sit down. "I've just had the most interesting call."

Ted glanced down at her notes then back at her, a smirk on his face. "So I see. You were awfully interested in what this fellow"—he turned the page around—"Ryan was saying. I thought I was going to have to pull out my unicycle and ride around in circles juggling cats to get your attention."

"You can do that?"

He sighed. "Tell me about the phone call, Lise."

Lise did, and he listened intently. "So," she said when she'd told him everything, "what do you think?"

Leaning back in the chair, he settled his hands in his lap. "Well, first off, I think our folks will be happy to hear Latagnier will have a new restaurant. You know how we Cajuns like to eat."

She chuckled. "True. Anything else?"

"You're talking about the funeral home, right? The one at

the edge of what will be the promenade?"

"Yes." Lise rose and walked to the drawing she'd posted on the wall just that morning. "I'm hoping having this new place to dine will cause other restaurants to test the waters." As Ted stepped up beside her, she turned to offer a smile. "Imagine what that sort of influx of diners will do for the Dip Cone. You may need to add staff and lengthen the hours of operation."

"Imagine," he said softly then pointed to the promenade, now colored by the red bricks that represented the existing cobblestone streets. This morning, on a whim, she'd played with an idea to put a few vendor stalls carefully disguised as architecture in strategic places along the promenade. "What are those?" he asked as he pointed to one.

"I thought the area might be well used as a street fair or some sort of art or antique show. I've seen this done to great success in other places. If you were to come up with a recurring thing, sort of like the First Monday Trade Days they do in Canton, Texas. It's a three-day open-air flea market held the weekend before the first Monday of each month. With something like that you could really boost tourism."

He looked at the map, but Lise had the strangest feeling Ted wasn't seeing it at all. Finally, he turned to face her. "My friends think I'm an idiot."

What in the world? "Why is that, Ted?"

"Because I prayed for you." He shook his head. "No, that's not right. I prayed about you." His gaze moved from her eyes to her mouth then back to her eyes. "I'm not making any sense, am I?"

Lise shook her head then rested her hand on the frame of the map. "I'm afraid not."

"That's because I'm an idiot." He tapped the map and seemed to be thinking about something. "I wasn't going to tell you until it's all final, but I had a closed-door session with the city council this morning."

"Oh?"

"Mm-hmm." He inched his hand closer to hers. "I summarized the whole thing. The promenade, the changes to the plan, all of it. Well, not the restaurant and these other things you've just mentioned, but all that I knew as of my last update."

Had he moved closer, or did it just seem so? Lise tried hard to concentrate. "And?"

"And they loved it. Not a single dissenting vote."

"Really?" Lise began to giggle. "You're not teasing me, are you?"

"Me? Tease?" He had moved closer—of that she was now certain. "Would I do that?"

Looking into Ted's eyes, Lise rambled the first words she could think of. "This is great news, Ted. I'm sure they were happy that their mayor came up with such a great plan."

"I couldn't take the credit for your ideas. I told the council it was your plan, and they approved it anyway." Ted paused. "Lise," he said in a deep voice, "have I mentioned my friends think I'm an idiot?"

She leaned in to hear him better. "Yes, you have."

"Care to know why?"

"Well." She felt his hand envelop hers. "I did ask, I think, a few minutes ago."

"Did you?" His hand was now at the back of her neck, warm and soft yet calloused and unyielding.

"They think I'm an idiot," he said, "because I didn't take the chance to kiss you when I first decided it would be a good idea."

"I see." Her stomach did a flip-flop when her gaze collided with his. "Well," she said, "here's your chance to prove them wrong."

So he did.

seventeen

"Lise, it's Ted. They caught the guy."

Lise leaned back against her pillows and pressed the phone to her ear. "Really?"

"I woke you up." He paused. "I'm sorry. Why don't you call me in the morning?"

"No, really, it's fine."

"You sure?"

She rolled onto her side and pushed the stack of novels away to check the bedside clock. Barely after eleven on a Friday night, and she'd fallen asleep reading. When had she become her mother?

"Go ahead and tell me what happened. Actually, first I'd like to know who it was." When Ted told her, she shook her head. "No, I don't recognize the name."

"He worked for one of the subcontractors." Ted paused, and she could hear the sound of dogs barking in the background. "Sorry. Anyway, I'm sure the chief will have more details, but the short version is that the guy's sister was on the cleaning crew that got the contract for the construction trailers. Seems as though she wasn't as careful as she should have been about where she kept her key."

"But why me?"

"Something about being repeatedly sanctioned for his lack of work ethic. Did you happen to complain to the supervisors about something like that?"

"Several of the subs seemed to stand around more than they worked." Lise sighed. "I might have mentioned that to them a few times."

"Hey." His voice was soft but firm. "That's your job. Don't feel bad about that."

"I know, but—"

"Lise."

She smiled at the sound of her name on his lips. "Yes?"

"Chief said he believes this is an isolated incident, but he's planning to see that the trailer's watched until he's satisfied that's the case. According to him, you can go back to work over there on Monday."

The implication of his statement hung in the silence between them. Feelings of relief and sadness warred inside her. While she was glad the man would no longer bother her, the clearance to return to the trailer meant she would also no longer work down the hall from Ted.

And that realization held more emotions than she could count.

"Lise?" This time his voice turned her name into a question. "You're awfully quiet."

She forced a chuckle. "I guess I am."

"It's a lot to take in. You okay?"

Was she? "Yeah, I'm fine. Much better now that I don't have an open police investigation with my name on it."

"Okay. Actually," he said, "I was just wondering why you would want to go back to that cold, drafty office when you could stay right where you are. Down the hall. From me."

Was that anxiousness she heard in the mayor's tone? "Well, I did move all my files out of the trailer. To go back, I would need to have someone help me move." She paused. "Next week is a short week, though, what with Thanksgiving coming up on Thursday. I wouldn't get much work done if I spent valuable time hauling things down the street."

"True. So it's settled. You'll stay until after Thanksgiving."

"Deal," she said, unable to keep the smile off her face.

Ted sighed. "Can I change the subject?"

"Sure."

"About this afternoon. The, um, kiss. You should know that's not like me. I just don't make a habit of kissing—that is, I just couldn't help it and, well. . ."

Her heart swelled. "Me, too."

"Yeah?"

His laughter held what sounded like relief mixed with happiness. At least Lise hoped she heard the same emotions that were going through her own being.

"Yeah," she said softly as she snuggled beneath her sheets.

"So I guess I should let you go back to sleep," he said.

"Actually," she said as she shifted positions, "I'm wide awake."

Two hours later, sleep still hadn't claimed her. Nor had she and Ted run out of things to talk about.

"Is it one o'clock already?" asked Ted. "I'm going to have a hard time getting up in the morning." He groaned. "And I promised my dad I'd help him with a project."

Lise rolled over and glanced at the clock. "Twelve after one, actually."

"Wow." He paused. "I could talk to you all night, but that's probably not a good idea. I stop making sense about two hours into sleep deprivation."

"Oh, really? And what do you sound like when you're not making sense? I think I've heard it before. Like over coffee at the Java Hut. No, wait. It was just yesterday in the kitchen at the office when you were attempting that Dean Martin imitation."

"Very funny."

She nodded. "Yeah, actually, it was. How did you ever learn to sound like him? I mean, a Cajun imitating an Italian?"

"Well," he said in his best Dean Martin voice, "it's a funny story. It all started with my uncle Guido Breaux."

And so they talked for another hour until she finally found sleep tugging at her.

"Lise, I'm going to tell you good night now."

Forcing back the cobwebs, she sat up. "I'm sorry. Did I fall asleep?"

"I'm not sure," Ted said, "but I think one of us was snoring."

❧

The sound of her phone awakened Lise from a deep sleep. Scrambling from her cocoon of blankets and pillows, she grabbed it and hit the green button.

"Well, hey there," she said as thoughts of her conversation with Ted came rolling toward her through the fog of sleep. "You must not need much sleep."

"Hey there, yourself."

The voice of her sister sent her bolt upright. The fog lifted and realization dawned. Susan had said nothing to acknowledge the likely-to-be-misunderstood statement. Lise realized she had two choices: Explain or ignore.

She went for the latter. "So how are things back home?" Lise said as casually as she could manage.

"Who is he?"

Lise stifled a groan and fell back onto the pillows. "The middleman, okay?"

There, she had said it. Lise drew in a breath and waited then slowly let it out.

"Well," Susan said brightly, "it's about time. Now about Thanksgiving."

"That's it?" Lise shook her head. "That's all I get after all the teasing and tormenting? 'It's about time'?"

"Oh, believe me, we will have a long discussion over coffee and apple pie while the family's watching football. Right now I'm trying to get the menu straight."

"Menu?" She shook her head. "Susan, didn't Mom tell you? I'm not going to be there this year."

"She did, but I figure after you hear my news you'll change your mind."

"Oh?"

Silence.

"Susan!"

Her sister's response sent Lise back two decades to their girlish conversations when Susan generally ended up dissolving in a fit of giggles. "All right," she said, "but if I tell you the news now, you have to promise you will change your mind and be at the table Thanksgiving Day."

"Oh, Susan, I don't know. I really need to—"

"This is family," she said. "Emphasis on *family*. It's not like your work won't be there on Monday."

Against her better judgment, Lise finally gave in. "Oh, all right, but I will likely have to bring paperwork with me, and I don't want a word from you on the subject."

"Promise?" Susan asked, her happiness evident.

Lise nodded. "Promise."

"Pinky promise."

"Susan!"

"All right." She paused. "I'm pregnant!"

"Oh, honey, that's wonderful!"

She gabbed with Susan until the phone beeped, announcing another call. A glance at the screen told her it was Ted Breaux.

"He's calling," she interrupted. "What do I do, Susan?"

"Who's—oh, *he's* calling. Well," she said in a maddeningly slow voice, "let him leave a message. You don't want him to think you're too available."

"Oh, please. Everyone in town knows that. Who could I possibly be dating?" The beeping stopped. "Too late. He hung up."

"Then I will do the same so you can, after a while, call him back." She paused. "Thank you, by the way."

"Thank me?" Lise swung her legs over the side of the bed and rose. The floor was cold, and so were her feet. "For what?"

"For agreeing to be there when we make the big announcement. I know I haven't always been the most supportive sister, and I certainly don't understand half of what you do as an architect, but I do appreciate you. And I love you dearly."

"Oh, Susie-Q, I love you, too."

After hanging up, Lise fought the urge to return to the comfort of her blankets, opting instead for a hot shower. By the time she'd dressed and made her way into the kitchen to fetch the coffeepot, she'd managed to shake the cobwebs caused by an incomplete night's sleep.

As the coffeepot gurgled to life, Lise heard her phone ring. She padded into the bedroom and caught it on the last ring, noting just before she placed the phone to her ear that the caller ID proclaimed Ted Breaux's name.

Smiling, she offered a bright greeting.

"Well, hello to you, young lady."

Lise nearly dropped the phone. "Who is this?"

"Oh, I'm sorry. Remember the fellow who said he'd help you with the millwork project downtown?"

The image of a spry, gray-haired fellow was quickly followed by confusion. "I do, but why are you calling from the mayor's telephone?"

He chuckled. "I reckon you'll figure that out soon enough. I was wondering if I might bring that fellow I was telling you about to meet you."

"The fellow? Oh, the carpenter." She reached for a mug and set it on the tile counter. "Yes, of course. I'll be in the office on Monday and Tuesday then out for the rest of next week."

"Yes, well, would it be too much of an imposition on your weekend to get together today?"

"Today?" She paused as the reminder of the value of old-timers and their advice came to her. "Sure, I'm free all day."

"Even better. What say I treat you to lunch for your troubles?"

"It's no trouble," she said, fully intending to get out of

anything other than a professional gathering of three people—

Until she arrived at the location of their meeting and found that the carpenter the old man had brought along was Ted Breaux.

His smile was broad. "Lise, I understand my father's been up to no good."

She looked from the tall Cajun to his companion. "Your father?"

The old man winked at her. "Guilty."

Her gaze returned to Ted. "What part do you play in all this, Mr. Mayor?" *And why didn't you mention any of this during our marathon phone call last night?*

Ted leaned toward her and brushed her cheek in a brief kiss that took her aback and then, to her horror, caused her to blush for the first time since junior high. "My role began as the innocent victim of a crafty old man's scheming."

"Hey," Ted's father said with a chuckle, "watch it."

"As I was saying, I started out that way, but once I figured out what he was planning, I decided for once he had a pretty decent idea."

"Oh?"

"Here's the short version: I'm a better-than-average carpenter, and my prices fit right into your budget for the bank renovation." He captured her fingers and held them. "The deal is you pay for the materials out of the budget and I throw in my labor for free."

His fingers tightened around hers, causing Lise to stumble over her question. "What—I mean, why?"

"Why?" He shrugged. "Actually, I have two reasons. The first is that I would be honored to be a part of putting back together the work that one of my ancestors did. Also, I'm not going to lie. I look forward to working with you."

The flames in her cheeks burned hotter. For a moment, she said nothing.

"Well, looks like she's got no more questions," Ted's father said. "Maybe we could take this meeting back to my son's place and continue it over steaks cooked out on the grill."

Somehow, before she could catch her breath, Lise was riding beside Ted Breaux IV in his Bubba-mobile while the man her sleep-deprived brain finally realized was Ted Breaux III followed.

"What just happened back there?" she finally managed.

Ted slid her a sideways glance. "What do you mean?"

"Well, just yesterday we, um. . ."

"Kissed for the first time?" he offered with a grin.

"Well, yes. And now you, well. . ."

"Kissed your cheek and held your hand in front of my father and whoever else might be watching?"

She nodded.

Another sideways glance. "I did, didn't I? Whoa, I'm really sorry, Lise." Ted cringed. "Man, I've never done that. I mean, I don't know what came over me. I didn't even realize. . ."

Lise reached across the expanse between them to capture his hand. "Don't apologize. That would be inexcusable."

"Inexcusable?" His grin returned. "We wouldn't want that, would we?"

"No," she said as she felt him squeeze her hand. "We wouldn't want that."

eighteen

Declining an opportunity to sit at Peach's table on Thanksgiving was difficult, but thinking of leaving Ted Breaux in Latagnier, harder still. From Saturday afternoon's impromptu barbecue to Sunday's after-church lunch at Peach's house, Lise spent most of her waking hours with Ted. Monday, at work, she found herself peering up occasionally to see if Ted might be walking by. By Tuesday, she'd given up the pretense of thinking Ted might be the middleman and started wondering if he might be *the* man.

Thankfully, she would have plenty of time to contemplate the question during her trip back home.

The time back in Houston did her good, as did seeing her family again. While in town, she was careful not to fall back into her drab ways lest Susan or Mother perform a fashion intervention. Thanksgiving Day was a much bigger affair than in years past, what with both sides of Susan's and her husband's families on hand for a celebration that included not only the big baby announcement but an entire dessert table decorated in a pink and blue theme.

On the day before Lise was to return to Latagnier, she finally had a conversation with Susan about the middleman.

"Ted sounds wonderful, but there's just one thing. Promise you won't marry him, Lise," Susan pleaded. "Or rather, promise you will think of him only as the middleman until the Lord tells you otherwise."

"I promise," she said, "at least until I'm sure."

The promise carried her through the weeks leading up to Christmas Eve when she stood with Ted in the center of the muddy, wet mess that would soon be the Latagnier Promenade. Since it was Christmas Eve, the job site was clear of all workers as of noon, when they'd been given bonuses and the rest of the week off.

In an hour she'd be in her SUV headed for Houston. Unfortunately, the prospect of spending the holiday away from Ted held little appeal.

"If I were a selfish man, I'd beg you not to leave today, Lise," he said. "But I'm not selfish, so I'm not going to say a word. No, that's wrong. Let me take you on a drive—just a short one—then I'll let you go." He paused to wrap his arm around her waist. "Thank goodness I'm not an idiot anymore."

Lise leaned into the embrace and stood on tiptoe. "Prove it," she teased.

So he did.

&

When he'd kissed Lise good and proper, he helped her into his truck and drove down toward the bayou. The weather was cold but not bone-chillingly so, and he hoped the clouds he saw on the horizon stayed put.

Bypassing his place, Ted turned the truck down the narrow dirt road that led to his favorite place on earth outside the chapel. Lise bounced with the truck, occasionally glancing over to offer a smile.

"We're here," he said as he applied the brake and shifted into park. "Come with me." He trotted around to lift her out of the truck, stealing a quick kiss before he set her on her feet. "I've got something I want you to see."

"What is it?" she asked as she reached over to entwine her hand with his.

Walking this way, hand in hand, made him feel like a million bucks. Now he truly understood what Bob and Landon had been telling him all along. He was an idiot.

As they reached the clearing, he paused. "See that over

there? The structure that looks like an Acadian home?"

"Yes, it's breathtaking."

He was looking at her, not the Breaux place. "Yes, breathtaking," he repeated.

Leading her to the doorstep, Ted reached into his pocket then unlocked the door. It swung open on hinges that he'd oiled just this morning.

"Come on in," he said. "Welcome to the former site of Latagnier School. Before that, it was the home of my great-great-grandparents. At least I think I got that right."

For a moment, he lost her to the beauty of the old place. Ted released her hand, and she wandered away, touching first this surface and then another. She said nothing. She did not need to. Finally, she returned to his side.

"I have no words," she whispered. "Except that I could stand here all day and just be."

"Just be?"

Lise nodded as her eyes slid shut. "Listen to the quiet, Ted. Isn't it wonderful? Like a dream."

"It is." He gathered her into his arms once more. "Yes, a dream," he repeated.

"Ted," she whispered against his chest, "have I ever told you about the middleman?"

He leaned away to look down at her. "No, I don't think you have. What's a middleman?"

Her smile was slow, her eyes falling shut once more as she rested her head back against him.

"Not what; who."

"All right, who?"

She shook her head. "It's not important."

❧

Time flew once the New Year's bells were rung, and in no time it was spring. It seemed as though the changes had barely been approved before construction on the Latagnier

Promenade was under way. Under Lise's expert supervision, the hardware store became a mercantile, the bank became a bookstore, and the funeral home became the first of four new restaurants on the promenade. And all of it happened in record time.

Any other project that came in under budget and ahead of schedule would have made Lise proud. Instead, every item that got marked as complete meant one less thing keeping her in Latagnier. Soon she would have to return to her life in Houston. How she would manage it, Lise had no idea.

In the weeks since their first meeting, Lise had become fast friends with Bliss Tratelli and Neecie Gallier, and they soon created a group of their own to keep one another accountable.

She would miss them terribly.

Lise sat in the middle of her bed, soggy tissues surrounding her like confetti. The project was all but complete. All that remained was a stack of paperwork and a return trip to Houston, and Latagnier would become another fond memory.

Her eyes puffy from the crying she'd done all afternoon between spurts of packing, she almost didn't answer the doorbell when it rang. Ted had seemed preoccupied the last week, so much so that Lise hadn't seen him for two days.

In a moment of clarity, she realized he must think that the kisses they'd shared were akin to those traded among teenagers at summer camp. Great fun but with nothing substantial to anchor them to love.

And yet she did love Ted Breaux. She'd figured that out way back at Latagnier School when they'd stood and listened to the quiet together. For her, however, there really had been no quiet that day. Set against the furious pounding of her heart was the quiet yet audible whisper of the Lord telling her she'd found more than the middleman.

Lise sighed and blew her nose on the last remaining tissue in the box then threw open the door. She'd be gone tomorrow, so what did it matter who stood on her porch?

"Ted."

"Don't go, Lise," he said as he dropped to one knee in the circle of porch light and offered up a tiny package wrapped in blue paper. "Stay. Be my wife."

"But you're the middleman," she said. "I can't possibly. . ." Lise shook her head and allowed Ted to drop the package into her palm. "Oh, who am I kidding?"

Finally, she said, "Yes."

epilogue

Theirs was a formal wedding with all the trimmings in Lise's church back in Houston. Her mother had a fit about everything except the bridal gown and cakes. Those items she left in the trusted hands of Bliss Tratelli and Neecie Gallier.

The pair had bonded with Mother and Susan over china patterns some weeks after the engagement was announced. The general assessment was that a significant amount of guidance would be needed to usher Lise into wedded bliss in a proper ceremony.

Thus, her gown was chosen for the way it accentuated the curves that her work clothes did not. Her hair was done with style and not convenience in mind, and since it was not yet Labor Day, she wore white shoes without her mother's consternation.

Of course, the reception went off as planned, and as far as anyone knew, the happy couple headed off to a honeymoon in some exotic location. That was what Lise expected, too, when she climbed into Ted's truck and headed east on I-10 at his side.

They got all the way back to the Latagnier city limits before she realized they wouldn't be getting on an airplane—at least not tonight. "I hope you don't mind, Mrs. Breaux," Ted said as he turned off the highway onto a road that had become more than a little familiar over the course of their courtship. "But the guys helped me plan for tonight."

The guys? "As in Bob and Landon?"

He gave her a who-else-could-it-be? look.

Lise snuggled against him. "Why would I mind?" she

asked as she resisted the temptation to ask any more about the night's plans.

A glow in the distance caught Lise's attention, and she sat up a little straighter. "What is that?"

Ted's grin warmed her to her toes. "That's where our dreams begin," he said. "Now put this on or you'll ruin the surprise." He handed her a handkerchief. "See that you tie it so you can't peek."

Lise obliged, her nerves jumping. What could her husband possibly have in store?

The truck lurched to a stop, and Ted's door opened then closed. A moment later, hers opened and she felt herself being lifted out of the truck.

"What are you doing?" she squealed. "Put me down."

He tightened his grip. "Not yet, Lise. It would ruin the surprise."

She endured jostling and a few sharp turns to end up being gently laid onto what felt like an air mattress. Was the man of her dreams going to take her swimming on her wedding night? Surely not.

And yet now that she was paying attention, she could hear the crickets and the rush of water. Bayou water. Inhaling, she savored the sweet scent of damp earth mingled with the clean smell of her husband's aftershave.

The combination was a heady mix.

Lips covered hers and remained until she was breathless. "I love you, Mrs. Breaux," her husband said, "and I wanted to start our life out right."

"Yes," Lise managed.

"So the guys helped me prepare the perfect memory for us." His lips moved from her mouth to her chin then to a spot behind her ear that made her toes curl. Warm fingers caressed her forehead then cupped her cheeks. "Keep your eyes closed until I tell you to open them."

"All right."

Again he kissed her. "Lise, we're building dreams together. I want tonight to be the first of a hundred—no, a hundred thousand—nights just like this. When we're old, I want this to be our place and our getaway. What do you say?"

She smiled and reached out to draw her husband near. He resisted, pulling her into a sitting position instead.

"All right," he whispered. "Take off the handkerchief."

"Ted," Lise said slowly as she took in the lantern, the canvas, and the sleeping bag. "Where are we?"

"Ah," he said, "we're camping. Isn't this great?" Ted nuzzled her ear, and Lise almost forgot about the mosquito coil burning a few feet from the sleeping bag.

"Camping."

"Mm-hmm."

"And the guys helped you with this?"

"You, Lise Breaux, are and always will be my first lady." Ted traced her jawline with his forefinger. "And, yes, they did. Now what say we start building those dreams, Mrs. Breaux?"

And the First Lady voted a hearty and enthusiastic yes.

A Letter To Our Readers

Dear Reader:
In order that we might better contribute to your reading
enjoyment, we would appreciate your taking a few minutes
to respond to the following questions. We welcome your
comments and read each form and letter we receive. When
completed, please return to the following:

Fiction Editor
Heartsong Presents
PO Box 719
Uhrichsville, Ohio 44683

1. Did you enjoy reading *Building Dreams* by Kathleen Y'Barbo?
   ❑ Very much! I would like to see more books by this author!
   ❑ Moderately. I would have enjoyed it more if

   _____
   _____
   _____

2. Are you a member of **Heartsong Presents**? ❑ Yes ❑ No
   If no, where did you purchase this book? _____
   _____

3. How would you rate, on a scale from 1 (poor) to 5 (superior),
   the cover design? _____

4. On a scale from 1 (poor) to 10 (superior), please rate the
   following elements.

   ____ Heroine   ____ Plot
   ____ Hero   ____ Inspirational theme
   ____ Setting   ____ Secondary characters

5. These characters were special because? _____

_____

_____

6. How has this book inspired your life? _____

_____

_____

7. What settings would you like to see covered in future
   Heartsong Presents books? _____

_____

_____

8. What are some inspirational themes you would like to see
   treated in future books? _____

_____

_____

9. Would you be interested in reading other **Heartsong
   Presents** titles? ❑ Yes ❑ No

10. Please check your age range:

   ❑ Under 18   ❑ 18-24
   ❑ 25-34   ❑ 35-45
   ❑ 46-55   ❑ Over 55

Name _____

Occupation _____

Address _____

City, State, Zip _____

Mississippi WEDDINGS

3 stories in 1

Romance rocks the lives of three women in Magnolia Bay. Meagan Evans's heart is torn between two men. Ronni Melrose meets a man determined to break down her defenses. Dani Phillips is caught in a raging storm—within and without. Can these three women ride out the wave of love?

Contemporary, paperback, 352 pages, 5³/₁₆" x 8"

Heart♥ong

Presents

Great Inspirational Romance at a Great Price!

Heartsong Presents books are inspirational romances in
contemporary and historical settings, designed to give you an
enjoyable, spirit-lifting reading experience. You can choose
wonderfully written titles from some of today's best authors like
Wanda E. Brunstetter, Mary Connealy, Susan Page Davis,
Cathy Marie Hake, Joyce Livingston, and many others.

When ordering quantities less than twelve, above titles are $2.97 each.
Not all titles may be available at time of order.